BURIED SECRETS –
WHERE IT ALL BEGINS

ISBN 979-8-9929483-5-6
Library of Congress Control Number: 2025917008

First edition, THE SECRETS, published 2019.
Second edition, BURIED SECRETS: A PSYCHOLOGICAL SUSPENSE NOVELLA, published 2023.
Third edition, BURIED SECRETS - WHERE IT ALL BEGINS: A SUSPENSE THRILLER, published 2025.

Edited by Deirdre Lockhart at Brilliant Cut Editing and Chelsea Lauren at Represent Publishing

Formatted and Published by Represent Publishing

Book Cover by Brittany Evans @ BEDESIGNS.CA

BURIED SECRETS – WHERE IT ALL BEGINS

A SUSPENSE THRILLER

S.F. BAUMGARTNER

FB PUBLISHING

AUTHOR'S NOTE

To all readers, especially residents and those familiar with the state of Florida, I wish to clarify that the town of Marian and the Mirror Estate are purely fictional creations for this series.

All characters and events depicted in this novel are born from my imagination. Any resemblance to actual people, living or dead, or to real-life events is entirely coincidental.

For Mr. Charles (Chuck) Fiorelli,

Whose gentle nudge and unwavering support inspired the journey to republish this new and expanded edition. Your belief in my work has truly made all the difference.

PRAISE FOR BURIED SECRETS - WHERE IT ALL BEGINS: BOOK 1

I felt that the author wove a story that had twists and turns with unexpected moments sprinkled here and there.

— DELPHIA, GOODREADS

They say that dynamite comes in small packages. This one was definitely loaded with plenty of information that will blow your mind.

— TAMMY, GOODREADS

What a great story! This had enough thrill and mystery to draw me in even though it was a short novella.

— MEGAN, GOODREADS

"Organized Crime Networks are billion-dollar businesses operating in many crime areas. Members of organized crime groups often share a common link, for example geographical, ethnic or even blood ties."

- Interpol

32 YEARS AGO

"Took care of the cop."

"Good. Found the evidence?"

There was a pause. "Not yet. Not anywhere in his house."

"Find it!"

No more needed to be said. They knew what was at stake.

CHAPTER 1

FINAL GOODBYE

SEATTLE

Dylan Roche didn't recognize half the people shaking his hand, and the ones he did spoke in hushed voices, careful not to say too much. He nodded, numb, as water dripped from the cemetery's oaks onto the mourners below. His black suit—borrowed from Tommy—fit well enough, though the sleeves hung a little too long.

After the final prayer, Fr. Jon approached. "Your mother always made time for Adoration before her shifts, even if it was just fifteen minutes. I believe her faith shone in a special way. You might be surprised how many lives she touched by being there."

"She was a wonderful woman." Mrs. Patterson from the apartment next door shook his hand. "Always so quiet, so polite."

Dylan nodded. "Thank you for coming."

"Dylan." Tommy appeared at his elbow as the last mourners drifted toward their cars. "You holding up okay?"

"Yeah." The word came out hoarse. Dylan cleared his throat. "Thanks for being here."

"Where else would I be?" Tommy straightened his tie. "Listen, my folks wanted me to tell you again, anything you need, just let us know. Mom's already made three casseroles for your freezer."

Dylan managed a smile. "Tell her I appreciate it."

They walked toward the parking area, gravel crunching under their feet. The cemetery was too quiet, like all sound had been muffled under wet wool. Dylan glanced back once at the grave, marked now only by a temporary placard. The headstone would come later.

"You sure you don't want to come back to our place?" Tommy asked. "Dad's grilling. Mom made that potato salad you like."

"I should head home. Sort through some things."

"Okey dokey." Tommy fished his keys from his pocket. "But seriously, don't be a hermit. Call me if you need anything. Even if it's just to talk."

About to respond, Dylan stopped when movement caught his eye. A woman stood beside a marble angel statue about fifty yards away, partially hidden by its wing. She wore a dark coat, her hair pulled back. From this distance, in this light...

His heart stopped.

"Mom?" The word slipped out before he could catch it.

Tommy followed his gaze. "What?"

Dylan blinked. The woman shifted a bit, and for one impossible moment, he saw his mother's profile. The same delicate nose, the same way of holding her head when she was thinking. But that was impossible. He'd just buried her.

"Dylan? What is it?"

He looked again. The woman was gone.

"Nothing." He rubbed his eyes with his palm. "Thought I saw... never mind. Just tired."

Tommy studied his face. "You sure you're okay to drive?"

"I'm fine."

But he wasn't. As they reached Tommy's car, Dylan couldn't

shake the feeling someone was watching him. The sensation crawled between his shoulder blades like a cold finger tracing his spine. He turned in a slow circle, scanning the cemetery grounds.

Empty.

"Let's go." Tommy got in his car. "See you at the reception hall."

All Saints' reception hall smelled like coffee and casserole. Dylan sat at a folding table, picking at a paper plate of food while neighbors, coworkers, and church friends shared memories of his mother. He should have been listening, should have been grateful for their kindness. Instead, he kept glancing toward the windows.

One older man approached with a firm handshake and a rough voice that carried unexpected tenderness. "I used to come into the restaurant every day—same booth, same order. Your mom was the only one who ever got it right. I wasn't always… the easiest customer. But she never flinched. Gave it right back when I needed it. In a good way. She had a way of making you feel seen."

"Thank you." Dylan smiled.

The man nodded. "Here's my card with my personal number. Take care now, young man."

After he walked away, Dylan picked up the card from the table. Frank Rogers, Attorney. He put it in his pocket and resumed pushing the food around his plate.

The stories painted a recognizable picture of his mother—kind, hardworking, reliable. But they also highlighted how little these people knew her. No one mentioned her late-night sketching, her rearranging the furniture when she was worried, or her humming while doing dishes.

"Dylan?" Tommy dropped into the chair beside him. "You're not eating."

"Not hungry."

"Mrs. Chen brought those little sandwich things you like." Tommy's eyes narrowed, the same look he'd worn in college when Dylan had struggled through calculus. "How much did you have to borrow?"

"What?"

"For all this." Tommy gestured around the room. "Funeral home, burial plot, catering. Your mom didn't have savings."

Dylan set down his fork. "I didn't borrow anything."

Tommy's eyebrows rose. "Come again?"

"Life insurance. I didn't even know she had a policy." Dylan reached into his jacket pocket and pulled out a folded check stub. "Check came in the mail two days ago."

Tommy took the stub and examined it. "Atlantic Mutual. Never heard of them." He frowned. "Did you file a claim?"

"No. It just showed up."

"That's weird, man. Insurance companies don't usually cut checks before you submit a death certificate and fill out their paperwork. Trust me, I've seen enough estate settlements to know."

Dylan shrugged. "Maybe someone at the hospital called it in. I don't know how these things work. The check cleared. And I looked. It's not one of those scams—once you sign here, you agree to this loan or some such nonsense."

"Still strange." Tommy handed back the stub. "You have all the luck, though. Remember that scholarship? The one you didn't even remember applying for?"

"Oh, come on." Dylan put his hands up. "Do you know how many of those applications I filled out? Mom was so worried the federal grant wouldn't cover everything. You can't expect me to remember every single one."

"No, but..." Tommy cuffed Dylan's shoulder. "Both times, money appeared right when you needed it most."

Before Dylan could respond, Mrs. Patterson approached with a covered dish. "Tuna casserole for later." She set it on the table. "And, honey, I wanted you to know your mother was proud of you. She used to brag about your job, how well you were doing."

"Thank you."

She patted his arm and moved away.

Dylan slid the casserole farther away, throat tight. His mother had been proud of a management trainee position that barely covered his living expenses.

"Ready to go?" Tommy pushed back his chair.

Dylan nodded. As they gathered their things, that watched feeling returned. He glanced toward the church entrance and froze.

A woman stood in the doorway, backlit by afternoon sunlight. Dark hair, familiar posture. She raised one hand, a wave of acknowledgment, then stepped back into the light and disappeared.

"Did you see that?"

Tommy looked toward the door. "See what?"

The doorway stood empty.

Dylan's pulse hammered in his ears. "Nothing. Let's go."

But as they walked to the parking lot, one thought rang clear: *Someone's watching. Someone who looks exactly like Mom.*

CHAPTER 2
COMMUNITY CARE

The insurance check stub lay beside Dylan's laptop, crisp and official-looking. Tommy's words from the funeral echoed in his mind: *That's weird, man.*

Everything seemed weird these days.

The numbers on his laptop screen blurred together, three red cells glaring like warning lights. His phone buzzed on the table. He rubbed the bridge of his nose before answering.

"Yes, I know rent is due on the first. I'm just asking for a little more time. My mom passed away a week ago. I'm still trying to get things in order."

"I'm sorry to hear that. I'll note your account and give you a little space. When you're ready, we can talk about next steps."

"Yeah. Thank you." Dylan disconnected the call and sank into his chair. His fingers tightened around the phone. The kitchen wall across from him would make a satisfying target. He could picture the phone shattering against the faded paint, plastic pieces scattering across the linoleum.

"Breathe through it, Dylan." His mother's voice seemed to whisper from the empty kitchen. *"Surrender to the Lord!"*

He crossed himself and prayed. *Lord, I surrender myself to you. Take care of everything!*

The tension in his shoulders began to ease. When he opened his eyes, the crushing weight in his chest had lifted, replaced by a quiet certainty that he wasn't carrying this burden alone.

He opened his laptop again, the red cells still glaring at him. The bills hadn't disappeared, but somehow, they appeared manageable now.

After graduating from college two years ago, he moved back in with his mom to save money and helped her during her cancer treatments. Now, her absence became a physical hollowness in his chest, a constant reminder she was gone.

He glanced toward the refrigerator, half expecting to see her studying the doctor's appointment magnet, lips moving silently as she confirmed the date and time. *"Pick up your socks!" "Put the dishes in the dishwasher!"* She used to yell at him for leaving things all over the place.

Now, the kitchen sink gave its own scolding. He pushed back his chair to clean up. His mom might not have bothered to decorate the apartment, but she'd kept her place neat and tidy.

As he turned on the faucet, running water triggered something deeper. Her final days in the hospital room flashed unbidden through his mind. The antiseptic smell, the beeping machines, the way her small frame seemed to sink further into the bed with each passing day. He'd held her hand as she slipped away, her fingers cold and fragile in his grasp.

"I'll take care of everything, Mom," he'd promised. *"Don't worry about anything."*

Shaking his head, he chuffed out a breath. How would he keep that promise? The medical bills alone were staggering, and her insurance hadn't covered everything. His credit card debt loomed large, and the rent was already late.

It had always been his mom and him. She'd worked hard as a waitress to support them. Time and time again, he remembered her kneeling by her bed at night to pray. They'd had happy days in the apartment, celebrating his significant events such as confirmation and graduation. She had been thrilled when he snagged one of the few coveted management trainee spots in the two-year program of a well-known regional property management company.

His phone buzzed, interrupting his reminiscing. Not wanting to answer any more calls from the landlord or loan officers, he checked the screen, expecting to swipe the decline icon. But Tommy's contact flashed. They had been best friends since grade school. They'd gone on to the same college but pursued different career paths.

"Yo," Dylan said.

"Hey, are you still moping around?"

"No, I don't mope around."

"Are you dressed? My guess is you're still in your shorts and T-shirt. It's past noon."

He patted his T-shirt. "So? I have time off until tomorrow. Bereavement leave."

"Yeah, I know. But really, how're you holding up?"

"Meh." The one syllable carried everything he couldn't articulate. How could he explain that he woke up every morning forgetting she was gone, only to remember anew each day? That he'd picked up his phone twice already to call her before realizing she wouldn't answer?

"Tell you what. Why don't you get dressed and come meet me for lunch? I have something for you."

CHAPTER 3
UNEXPECTED VISITOR

"What's this?" Dylan reached for the bulging manila envelope Tommy slid across the table.

They'd claimed a corner booth at Grind Coffee, their usual spot since college. The lunch rush buzzed around them: orders called out, espresso machines hissed, and conversations mixed with indie music. Dylan had ordered his usual turkey and Swiss, though he couldn't remember the last time he'd finished a meal. Everything tasted like cardboard lately.

"You forgot to check the basket at the reception." Tommy unwrapped his panini. "Lots of cards. Some with checks and cash."

Dylan's eyebrows shot up. "People actually do that?"

"Where've you been living, under a rock?" Tommy took a bite and grinned. "'Course they do. It's like... funeral etiquette or something."

Dylan opened the envelope. His breath caught. Bills and folded checks filled nearly half the space, along with a stack of sympathy cards. He pulled out a twenty, then a fifty. A check for thirty dollars from Mrs. Chen. Another check for a hundred from Rodriguez, probably from the family who ran the corner market where his mom sometimes shopped, though he'd never learned their first names.

"Oh my!" He lowered his voice. "How much do you think is here?"

Tommy shrugged. "Didn't count. But enough to help, I'd guess."

Dylan flipped through the checks and bills, his hands a little too careful, like one wrong move might turn a check into a notice. A couple of hundreds. A few fifties. More twenties and tens than he could count quickly. His throat tightened. These people—most of them barely knew his mother. Mrs. Patterson lived on social security.

"I can't take this," he whispered.

"What're you talking about?"

"These people don't have money to spare. Mrs. Patterson's husband died last year. She's likely struggling herself."

Tommy set down his sandwich and leaned forward. "Dude, they gave it because they wanted to. Because your mom mattered to them. You think Mrs. Patterson would've handed over fifty bucks if she couldn't afford it?"

Dylan fumbled with a check from Frank Rogers, the attorney who'd approached him at the reception. Five hundred dollars. His vision blurred.

"Besides," Tommy continued, "didn't you just tell your land-lord you needed more time? This might not cover everything, but it's gotta be close to your rent, right?"

Dylan nodded. A quick mental tally suggested this might cover most of his rent. Not enough to solve everything, but enough to breathe. Enough to call his landlord back with some-thing more than excuses.

"I just..." He folded the envelope and set it beside his plate. "Mom always taught me to stand on my own two feet. Taking handouts—"

"It's not a handout." Tommy's voice carried unusual firmness. "It's community. It's people caring. Your mom would've been the first person to help someone else in your situation."

That hit home. How many times had he seen his mother slip an extra five to someone short on their restaurant bill? Or bring groceries to elderly neighbors?

"Yeah." Dylan picked up his sandwich, his appetite returning. "You're right."

They ate in comfortable silence. The turkey tasted like turkey for the first time in days. He'd been surviving on coffee and whatever leftover casseroles he could stomach.

"So, Joanie's still making your life miserable?" Dylan asked.

"Get this—yesterday she made me reformat every number in the workbook to have comma style with zero decimals. Took forever. As if the client's going to back out of the audit because I left a few numbers unformatted.

"That's insane."

"Tell me about it. But hey, I passed the CPA exam. Just need to fulfill the experience requirements, then I'm outta there." Tommy checked his phone and winced. "Speaking of which, I better head back before she docks my pay for a long lunch."

They gathered their trash and headed outside. The afternoon sun warmed Dylan's face, the first time he'd noticed the weather in days.

"Thanks, man." He stopped beside Tommy's car. "For everything. Saving the envelope, lunch, just... being here."

"That's what friends do." Tommy punched his shoulder lightly. "Call me later, yeah? And don't spend all that money in one place."

Dylan waved as Tommy drove off, then started the six-block walk home. The envelope felt substantial in his jacket pocket, not just from the weight of the money, but from the weight of people caring. Maybe he wasn't as alone as he'd thought.

He was fishing for his apartment key when a voice behind him called out.

"Dylan Roche?"

Dylan turned. A man emerged from a sleek black sedan parked at the curb. Early sixties probably, with silver-streaked hair and a charcoal suit that cost more than Dylan's monthly salary. Everything about him screamed expensive, from his Italian leather shoes to the gold watch glinting at his wrist. He moved with the confident stride of someone accustomed to being the smartest person in the room.

"Yes. May I help you?"

The man approached. "Charles Townsend. I represent an interested party who'd very much like to meet with you."

Dylan's hand tightened on his keys. "I'm sorry, who are you exactly?"

"Of course." Townsend reached into his jacket and produced a business card and driver's license. "Townsend, Zimmerman & Associates. We're a law firm based in Orlando."

Dylan examined both documents. The license photo matched, and the business card felt expensive, heavy stock, embossed lettering. Still, every instinct his mother had taught him about stranger danger was firing.

"What's this about?" He handed back the ID.

"I'm afraid it's rather sensitive. Perhaps we could speak somewhere more private?"

A few neighbors were coming and going from the parking lot, but no one paid them any attention. Still, something about this whole situation felt surreal. Men in thousand-dollar suits didn't typically show up at his apartment complex.

"If this is about debt collection or—"

"Nothing like that." Townsend smiled. "Quite the opposite, actually. This concerns a family matter you may not be aware of."

Family matter? Dylan's pulse quickened. His mother had insisted they had no family left.

"I'm not sure what you mean."

"Mr. Roche, I realize this is unexpected. But I assure you, what I have to discuss will be very much worth your time." Townsend gestured toward Dylan's building. "Perhaps your apartment?"

Every rational part of Dylan's brain screamed no. Don't let strange men into your home. Don't trust people who show up unannounced with vague promises.

But another part of him, the part that had wondered his entire life about grandparents, cousins, anyone who shared his blood, whispered: *What if?*

"Can you at least tell me what kind of family matter?"

Townsend's eyes held something that might have been sympathy. "It's about your mother's family, Mr. Roche. About people who've been looking for her for a very long time."

CHAPTER 4

A GRANDMOTHER'S HOPE

ORLANDO

Aside from two other women praying quietly, no one was in the chapel.

Carol Marino lit a candle for the grandson she'd never met and whispered a prayer that he would forgive her family's sins.

She shifted on the wooden pew, a familiar ache settling between her shoulder blades. The pain had no medical cause. Dr. Green had confirmed that months ago. But guilt could manifest in surprising ways.

She rose and moved toward the candle rack near the side altar. Cloudy afternoon light filtered through stained glass, casting soft red and gold hues across the tile. Her fingers trembled as she fished folded bills from her purse, not from age, but from what she was about to set in motion.

Pausing before the statue of the Virgin Mary, she lit a single candle. The flame wavered, then caught steady. "Watch over him," she whispered. "Guide him here."

Beeswax and frankincense scented the air as she turned toward the sacristy.

"Ah, here you are, Carol."

Fr. Phil stood in the doorway of his small office, his familiar warmth grounding her as always. He pulled out a chair, gesturing for her to sit.

"So, what's so urgent?"

She settled into the seat, her back straight despite the phantom pain. The office felt like a sanctuary within a sanctuary. Dim light filtered through stained glass, books lined the shelves, and a hint of candle wax and old paper brought comfort.

"Charles located Maggie."

"That's wonderful news. You've found her, then." He smiled until he caught her expression. "What's wrong? Doesn't she want to see you?"

She drew a slow breath. Her fingers twisted together in her lap, knuckles white against still-smooth skin. "I was too late. She died. Cancer. Just last week."

Fr. Phil closed his eyes, bowing his head, muttering a prayer, presumably. "I'm so sorry. Did we miss the funeral?"

He sighed at her affirmation. "And the boy?"

The smallest smile tugged at her lips. "Yes. Dylan. Charles is meeting with him right now. He'll bring him here."

Fr. Phil leaned back in his chair, his weathered face showing the concern of a man who'd heard too many difficult confessions. "Is that wise?"

"I'm not thirty anymore, Phil. My heart's not getting any stronger." Her voice remained steady, but her gaze drifted to the window. "I need to meet my grandson. He needs to understand what he's inheriting."

"I understand your urgency. But he'll be overwhelmed. A family he never knew existed, sudden wealth, the... complexities of your history."

"Given our past, I doubt Maggie told him anything."

He nodded. "What if he wants nothing to do with it? With you?"

Her smile faded. "Then the Marino name dies with me." A pause. "And any chance of redemption dies with it."

"Now, now, there's always redemption."

She let out a soft, bitter laugh. "Charles says Dylan seems like a good young man. I have to believe I can help him see the right path forward."

"Just be careful. Sudden wealth changes people. And the weight of your family's legacy..." He spread out his hands. "That's a heavy burden for anyone."

"I know." She straightened, her voice gaining strength. "That's why I came to you. You've always been my anchor."

"Any wisdom I have comes from above, not from me."

Carol reached into her handbag, moving aside tissues, a leather prayer book, and her mother's silver rosary until she found what she sought. The cream envelope sealed with red wax bore no name, only the pressed image of the Marino family crest.

"Will you keep this safe?"

He accepted the envelope, studying the seal before placing it in his desk drawer. The lock clicked.

"It's for Dylan. My will covers the legal matters. but this... this is personal. In case he chooses to walk away."

"Of course." Fr. Phil's fingers drummed once against the desk. "What if he does choose to walk away?"

Her silence stretched long enough to answer the question they both feared.

CHAPTER 5
RESEARCH AND REVELATIONS
SEATTLE

Dylan studied the business card one more time, then the well-dressed stranger in his cramped living room.

"You must have a lot of questions." Townsend's voice was calm but precise, as if he'd rehearsed this moment.

Dylan gripped his knees. Something about this felt off, but what? The man had known his name. His apartment number. His mother's name.

Townsend continued. "Mrs. Marino will be more than happy to answer all of them."

Dylan had offered drinks, but Townsend had declined.

The story sounded simple enough. Carol Marino had retained Townsend's firm to look for her daughter, Margaret Marino. The search had led to him. Since Margaret had passed, Carol now wanted to get to know her grandson, whom she had never met.

Dylan shifted in his chair. The whole thing sounded like something out of a movie. But one question jumped out. "If my grandmother is still alive and wants to meet me, why send you? Why didn't she come herself?"

"Fair question. We need to be sure you are who we've been

looking for. And Mrs. Marino's health has recently declined. Her doctors have advised against a long journey. So, instead of coming to you, she'd like to invite you for a visit. If you accept, we'll fly you out to the estate." He stood. "Please think about it and contact me as soon as you decide. Not to sound cliché, but time is of the essence."

Dylan swallowed. His mother's voice echoed in his head: *If it sounds too good to be true...* But it didn't.

Townsend headed to the door. Dylan walked with him to show that his mom had raised a son with manners.

"Wait. When you said 'fly out,' what did you mean? Not to a foreign country, right? I don't have a passport." He pictured a helicopter or some offshore hideaway.

"Oh, don't worry! Just to Florida. No passport needed. And we've a chartered jet ready."

As soon as Townsend left, Dylan called Tommy. His friend didn't answer, so he sent a text. After pacing the floor, he sat to research the law firm and the family.

Charles Townsend and the firm, headquartered in Orlando, Florida, looked legit.

Still, something nagged at him. His mother had always taught him to be careful with strangers. He pulled out his wallet and found Frank Rogers's business card from the funeral reception. The gruff attorney had said to call if he needed anything.

Dylan dialed the attorney's personal number.

"Rogers here."

"Mr. Rogers, this is Dylan Roche. We met at my mother's reception yesterday."

"Of course, son. How are you holding up?"

Dylan explained Townsend's visit, keeping the details vague but asking if Rogers knew anything about the Orlando firm.

"Townsend, Zimmerman & Associates? Yeah, I know of them. High-end estate planning, corporate law. I hear they also have a criminal division. Charles Townsend's got a solid reputation. Why do you ask?"

"Just... being careful."

"Smart. Your mother raised you right. But if Townsend's representing someone, it's likely legitimate. He doesn't take cases that aren't worth his time."

Dylan thanked him and hung up, more confident but still wary. At least Townsend seemed legitimate. But that raised even more questions.

If Mom had ever mentioned her parents, he didn't remember. So now, he searched for Carol Marino. Too many results. Most women were too young. Several obituaries popped up.

He added his mother's full name, Margaret, and the city of Orlando to the search. That combination yielded some old articles.

The more he read, the more intrigued he became. If the articles were to be believed, then his mother had grown up wealthy. Everything he found said Carol and her late husband had been a very private couple. Ralph Marino had made public appearances for his import and export business, but little else was known.

Dylan scrolled through article after article, each one raising more questions. His phone's vibration against the table made him jump. A missed call from Tommy. Dylan called him back. After a recap, Tommy agreed to come over after work.

"So, what, you're royalty now?"

Having just finished explaining everything, Dylan waved off Tommy's question. "No, not me. My mom's family may be rich."

"Oh, come on. A private jet? If that doesn't count as rich, I don't know what does." He finished his beer and headed to the fridge. "So, what are you gonna do?"

"Not sure. It all sounds intriguing." Dylan shrugged. "The articles barely scratched the surface. Maybe they're just extreme introverts. Totally freaked out by people."

Tommy laughed. "Now I know you're related. You're just as private."

"I am not."

"You are. When did you tell me about your mom's cancer diagnosis? You weren't yourself. I had to pry it out of you."

"It wasn't anyone's business. She was—we were—dealing with it. Anyway, back to what we were talking about. What do you think?"

"Well, they're rich."

"Will you stop it?" Dylan groaned. "Think about it. My mom never told me anything about her family. I grew up believing they were all dead. If she had that kind of wealth, why leave? And why keep it a secret from me?"

"She told you near the end they were alive, right?"

"Yeah. But nothing more. I tried to ask, but she kept dozing off. The meds were strong. There's got to be a reason she hid her family from me."

"What, are they the Marino Mafia? You gonna kiss a ring or something? Like Michael Corleone?"

"Except Michael didn't stay out of the business. He became the don."

"That's beside the point. I say go. You always wanted to know your roots. And let's be honest, how many chances do you get to fly on a private jet?"

Dylan exhaled and closed the laptop screen, still open on the last article.

If this was real—if his mother had walked away from wealth, family, a whole life—then what had she been running from?

CHAPTER 6

SLEEPLESS NIGHT

Three hours of tossing and turning hadn't brought sleep, only more questions about why his mother never mentioned being rich.

Dylan rolled over, punching his pillow. A rich family, a private jet, an estate—and his mom had chosen a cramped apartment and diner shifts. Nothing about that made sense. Was it like Tommy had imagined? Or had her parents been abusive?

Giving up, Dylan padded into his mother's room in search of some kind of answer. Anything.

He hadn't touched her things. Not because he was avoiding it, but because he didn't know where to start. The room was as she'd left it, the faint scent of her grocery-store shampoo still clinging to the pillow. Like his own room, it was minimalist to the point of bare.

The closet held only a few items: a faded coat, two dresses that rustled when the heat kicked on, a pair of church shoes whose leather had been polished until it cracked. A small crucifix hung on the wall above her bed, its tarnished chain swaying slightly in the draft from the heating vent.

Her old laptop, a Christmas gift from him two years ago, sat propped against the nightstand. She'd never been tech savvy, as far as he knew.

He carried it to the kitchen table, which doubled as his desk. The plastic felt cool against his fingers as he opened it and powered it on.

Password?

Dylan stared at the cursor blinking in the empty field. What would she have used? He tried her birthday. Access denied. His birthday. Nothing.

Then it hit him—the same password she'd used for everything since he was a kid, the one she thought was so clever. He typed: Sunset325.

The desktop appeared, and Dylan frowned. Sunset325. He'd never understood why she'd chosen it. Their apartment faced east—they never saw sunsets. And 325 meant nothing to him. Just another mystery in a life full of them.

Unless it meant something after all. Something from the life she'd left behind.

His finger hovered over the trackpad. Mom's voice echoed: *Respect people's privacy, Dylan.*

But she was gone, and he needed answers.

They'd shared everything while he'd grown up—finances, schedules, even the same beat-up laptop until he saved enough for his own. Most of his friends had smartphones before middle school. He hadn't gotten one until he was seventeen, paid for with part-time job earnings and stubborn pride.

He clicked through the desktop folders. Nothing unusual. Bank statements. Grocery lists. A document labeled *Taxes_2022*. He kept looking.

Then he opened the photo gallery.

One folder held pictures from his high school graduation— his mother grinning ear to ear, eyes crinkled at the corners. His throat tightened as he scrolled through the photos. Another was from a friend's wedding. He remembered being shocked to see her dancing, like really dancing: tango, cha-cha, moves he hadn't known she knew.

There were plenty of candid shots too. Most featured just him, sprawled on the living room floor as a toddler, asleep at the dinner table, or blowing out birthday candles. She must have taken them when he wasn't paying attention.

But one folder made him pause.

The title was vague. Just a single letter: M. He clicked and held his breath as the page loaded.

Inside were only a handful of photos. Older, grainier. The people in them wore formal clothes. Suits. Silk blouses. Pearls. One might've been a gala or awards ceremony. Another showed a long banquet table, crowded with smiling faces in cocktail attire.

One woman, younger and elegant in a pale green dress, stood off to the side near an ornate room divider, her hand resting on a gleaming wooden credenza, her smile familiar.

Dylan leaned closer.

He pulled out his phone and opened his browser history. The article was still there. He tapped it, scrolled, and froze at the same image embedded in the story.

Same people. Same setting. Same smile.

The woman in the green dress was his mother.

But that couldn't be right. Could it?

The woman in the photo wore silk and pearls, like they belonged to her. His mom had owned two dresses—both from Walmart. He sank back in his chair, the discovery hitting him like a physical blow.

But now that he thought about it, she had always been particular about how rooms were arranged.

When he moved into his college dorm, she'd measured his desk and drawers ahead of time, bringing labeled bins and shelf risers like it was second nature. Back in middle school, she'd rearranged their living room for "better light flow" after borrowing a stack of home design books from the library.

Once, when he was about ten, he'd asked her what she would've been if she hadn't had him. She'd smiled and said, "I might've been an interior designer. Something quiet but beautiful."

He hadn't thought about that moment in years.

Now… what else hadn't she told him?

These weren't just strangers. They were the people his mother left behind.

And maybe, just maybe, she hadn't walked away at all. Maybe she'd been running.

CHAPTER 7
THE DECISION

The key around Dylan's neck felt heavier than it had any right to. Three grams of metal that might unlock everything his mother had hidden.

Dylan sat up, running his hands through his hair. The past week's crushing fog had lifted, but his chest still felt hollow every time he forgot to expect her voice from the kitchen. The photos from her laptop had replayed in his mind all night—silk dresses, champagne glasses, a life that didn't match the woman who'd raised him.

Still, something was different. A sense of purpose had replaced the aimless grief.

He lay back, staring at the ceiling, thinking of his grandmother. How many school projects had he fudged because he had no family tree to fill in? How many times had he envied friends with stories about crazy uncles and holiday traditions?

But that could change.

His fingers found the small key on its chain around his neck, a detail not even Tommy knew. Mom pressed it into his palm during her last lucid moment, her grip strong despite the morphine.

"At the estate," she'd whispered, her eyes more focused than they'd been in days. *"When you're ready... the key will show you everything."*

He'd tried to ask what she meant, but she'd drifted off again. The nurses had warned him the medication caused confusion, rambling. He'd assumed it was just that, drug-induced nonsense.

Now, those answers waited in Florida. All he had to do was get on a plane with a stranger and trust his mother's secrets wouldn't destroy him.

Time to move.

Dylan pushed himself out of bed, made coffee with shaking hands, and dialed his boss. Ken picked up after two rings. Dylan explained the situation, said he might need a few extra days. Ken didn't hesitate.

"Take whatever time you need," he said. "And listen, this won't hurt your shot at going permanent when the program ends. Your reviews have been solid. Everyone likes working with you. Just... if you need to talk to someone, let me know. We've got grief counselors on retainer."

"Good to know. Thanks."

He hung up, stared at the phone a second longer, then retrieved Townsend's business card from his wallet. The raised lettering caught the morning light.

He turned it over once, then dialed the cell number written by hand.

"Townsend."

"Mr. Townsend, this is Dylan Roche. I've made my decision."

A pause. "And?"

Dylan's thumb found the key through his shirt. "I'll come. When do we leave?"

"Excellent. I can have a car pick you up in two hours. Pack light, anything you need can be provided."

Dylan hung up and scanned his cramped apartment. In

twelve hours, he'd be in Florida. By tomorrow night, either he'd have the family he'd always wanted, or he'd understand why his mother spent twenty-five years running from them.

He pulled out his duffel bag and started packing.

His mother had kept one secret for twenty-five years. Whatever waited for him in Florida, he was about to walk straight into it.

CHAPTER 8

FIRST MEETING

ORLANDO

Dylan's eyelids snapped open to unfamiliar luxury, leather seats, mahogany trim, the hum of jet engines. For a disorienting moment, he'd forgotten where he was. Then reality crashed back: private jet, mysterious family, a grandmother who might hold answers to questions he'd carried his entire life.

"Dylan, Dylan."

"What?" He blinked, trying to shake off the fog of sleep.

Townsend hovered his hand in midair, poised to tap Dylan's shoulder. "You should buckle up. We're landing soon."

Dylan shifted and obeyed, his stomach tightening. "I could get used to this way of traveling. Sure beats flying coach. Is the estate in Orlando?"

"Not exactly. It's in Marian, a town about a forty-five-minute drive away. The closest airfield is in Orlando."

Beyond the small window, the Florida landscape unfolded, sprawling developments, highways cutting through wetlands, the occasional glint of water. His mother had grown up down there somewhere. Had she ever looked out a similar window, wondering if she'd made the right choice to leave?

The plane touched down with barely a bump. Within minutes,

they were walking across hot tarmac toward a sleek black vehicle. A chauffeur in a crisp uniform stood beside the open door.

"Mr. Roche." The driver nodded. "Welcome to Florida."

Dylan slid into the back seat, the leather cool against his skin despite the humid air outside. This was really happening. No going back now.

"Nervous?" Townsend asked as they pulled away from the airfield.

"Should I be?"

The lawyer smiled. "Carol's been looking forward to this for a long time."

They didn't talk much. Townsend returned to his phone, fingers flying across the screen with an urgency at odds with a family reunion. Dylan studied the man's reflection in the window. Something about Townsend didn't quite fit—too polished, too careful with his words.

The landscape changed from highway sprawl to two-lane roads winding through older neighborhoods. Spanish moss draped the oak trees like tattered curtains, and many houses must've been standing since before his mother was born.

"We're entering Marian now," the driver said.

A weathered welcome sign appeared:

Welcome to Marian – Where Tradition Meets Tomorrow.

"Charming," he murmured, though something about the slogan felt forced, like trying too hard to convince visitors the town was more than it appeared.

Main Street stretched before them, a collection of old brick buildings housing antique stores, cafés, a barbershop with a striped pole, and a diner with a chalkboard menu listing the day's specials. Strings of white lights crisscrossed overhead, giving the street a festive air even in broad daylight.

A few people on the sidewalks turned to watch their car pass, their expressions unreadable. But he caught something in their eyes. Curiosity? Or something else?

"Do people know who I am?"

"Small towns talk. Give it a day or two. Everyone will hear about you."

He shifted. The feeling of being watched was starting already, and he hadn't even reached the estate.

"Almost there," the driver announced. "Just around the next bend."

Dylan's breath caught as they rounded the curve. The estate sprawled before them like something from a movie, not as massive as the Biltmore, but impressive enough to make his Seattle apartment and his mother's waitressing shifts feel like they belonged to a different world.

Three main buildings were visible: a grand main house with columns and wraparound porches, and two smaller structures set back among the trees.

"The main house is straight ahead of us." Townsend pointed. "The building in the back that you see coming in houses the restaurant and staff quarters. Once we turn, you won't see it. The one on the right is the guesthouse."

Trees lined the drive like sentries, their branches forming a natural canopy that filtered the sunlight into dancing patterns. They approached the main gate, replete with security measures, cameras mounted on posts, a keypad system, and sensors built into the gate itself.

"Lots of security for a family estate."

"Carol values her privacy."

The driver punched in a code and waved at one camera. The gates swung open, and the vehicle rolled up the circular drive toward the main house.

"Here we are." Townsend pocketed his phone.

The chauffeur was out and opening Dylan's door as soon as the car had fully stopped. "Mr. Roche."

"Thanks." Dylan stepped out, hit by the humid air and the scent of jasmine and fresh-cut grass. Everything felt larger than life, from the towering columns to the manicured gardens stretching in every direction.

As they approached the front entrance, the double doors opened as if by magic. A man in his sixties appeared, tall, distinguished, with the kind of posture that suggested military training or years of formal service.

"Mr. Charles." The man nodded, then turned to Dylan. "You must be Mr. Roche."

"Yes. Dylan will do." He extended his hand.

The man hesitated before taking it, and during that brief handshake, his eyes seemed to catalog every detail about Dylan. "I'm the majordomo. Max, at your service."

"I'm sorry, major... what?"

"Majordomo. Like a property manager." Max's bearing suggested the title carried more weight than his explanation.

"Thanks, Max. Ms. Carol is waiting in the living room, I assume?" Townsend asked.

"She is indeed. Come this way, please."

Stepped inside, Dylan might as well have entered another world. The marble entry floor gleamed beneath a crystal chandelier that probably cost more than his annual salary. Antiques in glass cases lined the walls, and every piece of furniture, every drape, every rug spoke of old money and careful curation.

His mother had walked these halls. Had grown up surrounded by this wealth.

His chest tightened.

Townsend murmured, "Basically a butler." He tipped his head in Dylan's direction. "Impressive, isn't it?"

"It's... a lot."

They stopped beside a set of wide doors. Through the gap came the soft clink of china and the rustle of fabric.

"Here's the living room." Townsend gestured. "After you."

Dylan's heart hammered as he entered the room. A woman in a casual blouse and slacks rose from a wingback chair, and time seemed to stop.

She looked like his mother. This woman was older, hair dyed brown, minimal makeup, and few wrinkles. The bone structure, the way she held herself, even the tilt of her head was familiar enough to make his throat close.

"You must be Dylan." She smiled, her voice carrying a genuine-sounding warmth.

"Dylan, this is Carol, Mrs. Marino. Your grandmother." Townsend made the introductions. "Carol, yes, this is Dylan."

Once she had a chance to look at him, she gasped, one hand rising to her throat. "Charles, you see it?"

The lawyer glanced between them. "The resemblance? Yes."

Dylan had never heard anyone say he resembled Mom, but standing here, seeing Carol's reaction... Well, maybe he'd never had the right person to compare himself to.

"May I?" Carol opened her arms.

For once in his life, Dylan was tongue-tied. He managed a nod and stepped into the embrace.

She barely came up to his chin, smaller and more fragile than his mother had been, but her hug was firm and warm.

When they parted, a young boy hovered in the doorway as though trying to decide if he should interrupt.

Carol's eyes glimmered. "I know you must have questions. But let's get you settled first. We'll have plenty of time to talk." She beckoned to the child. "This is Sean, Max's grandson."

The boy bounded forward with the unselfconscious energy of youth.

"Hi, I'm Dylan." Dylan bent forward. "How old are you?"

"I'll be ten in forty-four days."

Dylan couldn't help but smile. Only kids count down to their birthdays like that.

"Sean, would you like to show Dylan to his room?" Carol asked. "I need to discuss a few things with Mr. Charles."

"Sure!" The boy grabbed Dylan's arm. "Just follow me. You might get lost, otherwise. This place is huge."

"I bet it is." Dylan glanced back at Carol and Townsend, catching the tail end of a meaningful look between them. "Don't want to get lost on my first day."

CHAPTER 9

PAINTED EYES

The portraits lining the grand staircase seemed to track Dylan's every step, their painted eyes following his progress with an intensity that made his skin crawl. He'd heard about the Mona Lisa effect, but this felt different, more personal, as if these long-dead Marinos were weighing his worthiness to walk their halls.

"So, are you really her grandson?" Sean asked as they climbed the grand staircase.

"I think so. I hope you don't work here."

"Nah, Grandpa does. Grammy helps my mom at the restaurant. Ms. Carol lets me hang out here all the time, though. She's really nice. My mom cooks for her." The boy's voice dropped to a conspiratorial whisper. "Grandpa says Ms. Carol spoils me like the grandson she never had. Maybe that'll change now that you're here."

They passed an endless row of doors. Sean provided running commentary, his voice echoing in the high-ceilinged hallway. "This is a linen closet. That's a bathroom. There's like six of them just on this floor."

Dylan only half listened, studying the nameplates beneath each portrait. The dates stretched back over a century; Marinos who'd built this wealth, this legacy. Had his mother walked past these same faces every day of her childhood, knowing she was supposed to carry on their tradition?

The boy stopped, checked both ways down the corridor, then dropped his voice to a whisper. "Grandpa told me once this used to be your mother's room."

Dylan's breath caught. "Think I can take a look?"

"Just be quick. Grandpa's rule is no touching anything."

"Okay." His hand found the key hanging around his neck as he approached the door. With Sean keeping watch, Dylan turned the handle and pushed the door open just wide enough to slip inside.

He'd stepped into a time capsule. A canopy bed dominated the space, its burgundy curtains tied back with silk cords. Everything was elegant but warm—a vanity with an ornate mirror, a reading chair by tall windows, and built-in bookshelves filled with out-of-date teenage favorites mixed with classic literature.

But the details made his chest tighten. Cosmetics still

arranged on the vanity as if she'd just stepped out. A sweater draped over the chair's arm. A pair of riding boots by the closet door. His mother must've left in a hurry and never come back—and yet, all this remained as it had been then.

He moved closer to the vanity, careful not to touch anything. Among the bottles and compacts was a framed photo, his mother as a teenager, laughing at something outside the camera's view. She appeared so young, so carefree. So different from the careful, watchful woman who'd raised him.

The key around his neck seemed to grow heavier. Had his mother left something here for him to find?

"Dylan?" Sean's whispered voice carried urgency. "Someone's coming."

Dylan backed out of the room, pulling the door shut as footsteps approached farther along the hall. Max appeared, carrying fresh linens.

"Ah, there you are. Everything all right?"

"Sean was just showing me around." Did his voice sound casual enough?

Max's gaze flicked to Dylan's mother's door, then back to Dylan's face. "I see. Well, Sean, perhaps you should show Mr. Dylan to his room now. I'm sure he'd like to get settled."

"Sure thing, Grandpa." Sean tugged Dylan's sleeve. "Come on. It's just a couple doors down."

As they walked away, Dylan caught Max watching them in his peripheral vision. Had the man seen him come out of his mother's room? And if so, what would he do about it?

"Here it is." Sean threw open the door with a flourish.

Dylan let out a low whistle. "You could fit my entire apartment in here." A king-sized bed—were those silk covers?—seemed lost in the massive room, where the other elegant furniture was arranged in perfect harmony.

"They cleaned this room earlier," Sean told him.

A citrus and fresh-flower scent lingered. "This is incredible."

"Wait till you see the best part." Sean rushed to a pair of glass doors and threw them open. "You can climb down from here to the gardens without going through the house. I do it all the time when I want to sneak out to the gazebo."

Dylan stepped out onto the private balcony, and his breath caught in his throat again. To his left, formal gardens created geometric patterns of color and texture around a serene pond that reflected the late afternoon sun. A gazebo nestled among the landscaping, partially hidden by ancient oak trees draped with Spanish moss. To the right, another building set back among the trees.

The beauty of it all made him forget why he'd come. A strange peace settled over him, as if this place had been waiting for his return.

I belong here.

Startled, he shook his head and muttered under his breath, "No, I don't."

"You said something?"

"Nothing important." But even as he said it, movement near the gazebo caught his eye.

He turned toward it, eyes narrowing. A shadow had slipped between the trees, too quick and purposeful to be random movement, too human-shaped to be an animal. "Did you see that?"

Sean followed his gaze, squinting against the sun. "See what? A squirrel?"

Hadn't Dylan glimpsed a woman? He shook his head. Maybe he was seeing things. Everything—his mother's death, the mysterious family invitation, that preserved room down the hall —must be making him paranoid.

"Near the gazebo. Someone was there."

"Probably one of the groundskeepers. They're always working around the gardens."

"Yeah. Probably." But his instincts said otherwise. The figure moved like someone trying not to be seen, and when he'd looked directly at the spot, they'd vanished.

He was just tired. It had been a long day, an emotional flight, and now he was in a strange place surrounded by family he'd never known existed. Of course, his imagination would be working overtime.

But as he glanced back toward the gazebo, he couldn't shake the feeling someone had been watching him. Someone who didn't want to be seen.

The boy pointed toward the pond's far side. "See? Way back there, a path takes you to a private beach. On the left is the garden. That building on the right is the guesthouse, and the one straight ahead is a restaurant. My family lives above it. Well, the household staff."

"As we came in, I saw a sign directing people to the restaurant. Your parents own the place? Or just work there?"

The kid shrugged, clearly not sure about the business arrangements. "I don't know. My mom is the chef. My dad is, like, a manager. You'll meet them soon. You won't want to leave once you taste her cooking."

Dylan's stomach chose that moment to growl. He'd barely eaten since morning, after all. "I'm more hungry than tired. Where's the kitchen?"

The boy giggled. "You don't need a kitchen. Let's go to the restaurant."

Sean tugged his sleeve, oblivious to Dylan's growing unease. "Wanna see something really cool? A tunnel connects all the buildings. We could go through it to check out the restaurant, and you could meet my mom and dad."

Dylan forced himself to focus on the boy's eager face. Whatever or whoever had been near the gazebo was gone now. "A tunnel? That does sound cool."

Still, as they headed back inside, he couldn't resist one more glance toward the trees. The shadows seemed deeper now, full of secrets he was only beginning to uncover.

And somewhere in those shadows, Dylan was certain, someone was still watching.

CHAPTER 10
HIDDEN PASSAGES

"This tunnel is amazing. You can just go back and forth even if it rains or snows outside." Dylan strolled alongside Sean through the underground passage connecting the buildings. The smooth stone lining the walls and soft lighting made the space feel less like a basement and more like a secret castle corridor.

"I've never gotten to see snow, but yeah, it's good when it rains or when it's super hot out." Sean swung his arms, his steps wide, his voice echoing in the enclosed space.

Dylan touched a wall. Had his mother used this tunnel as a child? Had she run through here with friends or walked alone when she needed to escape whatever had driven her away?

The tunnel opened into a basement, and they climbed a set of stairs that brought them into the restaurant's main dining area.

Lorraine's Kitchen wasn't what he had expected. Instead of a formal restaurant, it felt more like a cozy bed-and-breakfast dining room, small, warm, and lived-in. A faint scent of garlic and herbs lingered, mixing with something sweet that made his mouth water.

With the lunch rush over, only a handful of tables were occupied, mostly by what looked like locals. At a corner table, two elderly men in work shirts paused their conversation to eye Dylan. A woman with gray hair sitting alone near the window glanced up from her coffee and did a double take, her eyes widening.

"That's him," she whispered to the waitress. "Maggie's boy."

The name hit him like a physical blow. These people had known his mother.

Oblivious to the attention, Sean led Dylan toward a man busy at the register. "Daddy, this is Dylan, Ms. Carol's grandson."

The man stopped what he was doing, wiped his hands on his apron, and offered a handshake. In his thirties, he possessed the lean build of someone who worked on his feet all day and the easy smile of a man comfortable in his own skin.

"Nice to meet you, Dylan. We've been hearing about you. I'm Connor." His handshake was firm and genuine. "You've got a good tour guide here."

"That I do." Dylan ruffled Sean's hair despite the boy's protests. "He's been showing me around."

"Have a seat anywhere you like. Lorraine will fix you something special."

Instead of choosing a table, Sean grabbed Dylan's arm. "Come meet Mom and Grammy first."

The kitchen was like watching a master class in action. Lorraine moved between the stove and prep counter with the fluid efficiency of someone who'd been cooking professionally for years. With flour-dusted hands and a warm smile, she immediately put Dylan at ease. Her mother, who introduced herself as Kate, worked beside her, an older, slimmer version of Lorraine with silver hair secured in a practical bun.

Oven mitts rested on a counter near cooling racks filled with fresh bread. Someone had left a radio playing soft jazz in the kitchen, which, combined with the refrigeration equipment's gentle hum, provided a comforting background sound.

"Ms. Carol was so excited when she told us you were coming." Lorraine didn't miss a beat as she stirred something that smelled incredible. "The way she was going on, I thought she'd throw a big party and I'd have to cook for an army!" A slight frown crossed her face. "Come to think of it. She hasn't had any big gatherings for a long time, though the company does have me cater their business events quite often."

"Stop your yakking." Kate huffed out affectionate exasperation. "Dylan's probably starving after that long flight. We'll have plenty of time to catch up later. What sounds good to you, Mr. Dylan?"

"Just a sandwich would be fine." Although the aromas in the kitchen were making him reconsider.

Lorraine crossed to her prep counter, displaying house-made everything, chicken still steamy from roasting, vegetables that must've been picked that morning, bread right out of the oven.

"How about my chicken salad? I make it with roasted chicken, fresh herbs from the garden, and a touch of my grandmother's secret seasoning."

"That sounds perfect."

Every movement precise but natural, she seasoned and tasted, selected the perfect pieces of lettuce and sliced tomatoes. This wasn't just cooking—it was artistry born from years of experience and genuine love for the craft.

Sean directed him to a window table, settling in across from him with the familiarity of someone who considered this his second home.

"So tell me about these secret places you mentioned earlier." Dylan kept his voice casual, despite his growing interest. The key around his neck seemed heavier with every passing hour. He must find what it might unlock.

Sean's eyes lit up at an adult interested in his discoveries.

"Oh man. There's so much cool stuff. Like, there are rooms in the main house nobody uses anymore, and some of them are locked up. And Grammy Kate told me there used to be hidden passages for servants to move around without being seen by guests."

"Hidden passages?" Dylan folded his hands on the table and leaned forward. "Like secret doors?"

"Yeah! I've been trying to find them forever." Sean's voice dropped to a conspiratorial whisper. "I heard Grandpa talking to Ms. Carol about it once. He was saying something about peeling paint and a hidden door that needed to be fixed."

Dylan's pulse quickened. "Do you remember what they said?"

Sean scrunched up his face, trying to recall. "Grandpa was worried about the paint peeling and someone might see the door's outline. Ms. Carol said something like, 'Just touch it up. No one goes in that part of the house, anyway.'"

"Which part of the house?"

"I think... the old wing? Near where the library is?" Sean bobbed his head, his enthusiasm building. "I've looked everywhere I can think of, but I haven't found it yet. Grandpa says I'm too curious for my own good."

Dylan's hand moved to the key beneath his shirt. Could it open whatever was behind that hidden door? "Have you tried looking for unusual markings or anything that might show where the door is?"

"I've checked for cracks and stuff, but those old walls have lots of cracks." Sean paused as his mother approached with Dylan's lunch. "Mom makes the best chicken salad in Florida. Maybe the whole world."

Lorraine set down a plate straight from a food magazine, accompanied by house-made chips and a cup of fruit salad with fresh mint.

"Don't let him exaggerate too much." She shook a finger at

them, though her cheeks flushed. "But I do use my grandmother's recipe. She taught me that the secret is in the balance, not too much mayonnaise, fresh herbs instead of dried, and always roast your own chicken."

Dylan took a bite and nearly groaned with pleasure. Sean hadn't been exaggerating. The chicken was perfectly seasoned and tender, the herbs bright and fresh, and the bread's subtle sweetness complemented everything.

"This is incredible." He meant it. "I can see why people come from town to eat here."

"See? Told you!" Sean practically bounced in his chair.

As Dylan ate, Sean chattered about the estate's mysteries, but Dylan's mind was racing. A hidden door with peeling paint somewhere near the library. His mother's key, which had been important enough for her to press into his palm with her dying breath. The preserved room upstairs, a veritable shrine to secrets.

Everything was connected somehow. He was sure of it.

After the sandwich and a piece of apple pie, somehow even better than the chicken salad, Dylan thanked Lorraine and made plans with Sean for a more complete tour later.

"I think I'll walk back," he told Sean as they reached the restaurant's entrance. "Get some fresh air and maybe explore those gardens you mentioned."

"Want me to come with you?"

"Maybe later. I just want to clear my head now."

As Dylan stepped outside, the warm air formed a humid embrace, but that familiar sensation crept up his spine again, the weight of unseen eyes watching his every move. The formal gardens stretched before him, half in shadow as the afternoon sun angled lower, creating pockets of deep shade between the hedges.

He didn't mean to explore, but his feet carried him toward the maze of pathways and hidden alcoves. Behind him, the main house loomed silent and watchful, its windows reflecting the dying light like dozens of eyes.

And somewhere in those shadows, in the gardens, in the hidden passages Sean had described, in the locked rooms of his mother's childhood home, answers were waiting.

The key around his neck felt warm against his skin as he lost himself in the garden, leaving the safety of the open lawn behind.

CHAPTER 11
CARVED IN TIME

Each step down the garden path felt like slipping deeper into a place that remembered more than it revealed.

His mom walked these same paths. The gravel crunched beneath his shoes. The scent of freshly clipped boxwood mingled with something sweeter, roses, maybe, and the earthy trace of damp soil that spoke of recent rain and careful tending.

Did she love it here? Or did all this perfection feel like a prison?

He passed rows of zinnias and geraniums arranged in patterned beds, framed by low hedges that might've been trimmed daily. The symmetry reminiscent of the formal gardens at the Biltmore Estate played out like a painting brought to life. But his mother had grown up with this as her backyard, not a tourist destination.

She had all this, and she chose their cramped apartment instead. Why?

Here, though, nature had begun to reclaim the edges. Vines spilled over onto the walkway. Cracks had formed in the path where tree roots pushed upward. The farther he went, the more the manicured order gave way to something older, wilder.

A breeze stirred the leaves overhead, carrying their whispered secrets. He paused beneath a wrought iron arbor draped in climbing roses, their petals browning at the edges. The filtered light turned everything golden green, creating a cathedral of natural beauty.

He ran a hand along the ivy-covered archway, his fingers finding a rusted hinge beneath the leaves. A lantern maybe? Or a sign? Evidence of the estate's grander days when staff moved through these gardens serving elaborate parties.

The key around his neck pulsed with each heartbeat. *What did you want me to find, Mom?* His hand found the chain, rubbing the slight metal weight through his shirt. *You were so scared, so desperate. What were you trying to tell me?*

Up ahead, the path curved around a fountain with a moss-covered basin. Water still trickled from a lion's mouth carved in weathered stone, but the edges were chipped and worn down by time.

Did you make wishes here as a little girl? He studied the lion's face. *Did you think your dreams would come true?*

Something was peaceful about this spot, and yet something was off about it too. Like standing in a place where important conversations had happened, where decisions had been made that changed everything.

Beyond the fountain was a clearing with a gazebo, and his breath caught. This was where he had seen the shadow. The white paint was pristine, clearly maintained with the same care as everything else on the estate, but morning glory vines had been allowed to climb the railings in controlled abundance, creating a romantic canopy of green and purple blooms.

Beautiful. The kind of place where lovers would meet in secret.

Dylan stepped inside, and the floorboards groaned beneath his feet. Dust motes danced in the afternoon light filtering through the lattice. In the dust near the railing, faint smudges stood out; boot prints, maybe.

Someone had been here recently. But who?

He moved around the perimeter, scanning every surface. If his mom and dad spent time here, maybe they left something behind. Some proof they were happy, even if it didn't last.

There. Carved into the wooden railing, barely visible beneath years of weathering, were letters. His heart hammered as he knelt and brushed away the dirt.

MAM 🤍 MLR

Wow! Mom and Dad. His vision blurred. Margaret Anne Marino loves Michael Leon Roche. They were so young, so hopeful. Did they know then that they'd have to run? Did they know their happiness wouldn't last?

He traced the letters with one finger, imagining them here together, believing their love could overcome anything. The pain in his chest was sharp and sweet, grief for what he'd lost, but joy at this proof of their happiness.

The gazebo was well maintained. Why hadn't anyone sanded away the initials? Maybe they just couldn't erase her completely. *They missed you too, Mom!*

He pulled the key from around his neck, the filtered light caressing it. Maybe she hid something here. Something she wanted him to find.

Come on. There has to be something. He searched methodically, running his hands along railings, checking for loose boards. The key fit nowhere, but he kept trying every crevice and gap. She wouldn't have given this to him for no reason. There had to be a reason.

A sound made him freeze, careful, deliberate footsteps trying to move through the underbrush.

That wasn't a groundskeeper.

Through a gap in the lattice, he glimpsed movement near the tree line. A figure in dark clothing, partially hidden behind an oak tree. Too far away for details, but human. Watching.

The cemetery. His blood turned to ice water. Same posture, same way of moving. Either he was losing it, or someone followed him from Seattle.

"Hello?" Dylan called out, his voice steadier than he felt. "I can see you there."

The figure shifted, and he caught a clearer view. Dark hair, average height, long coat despite the Florida heat. Then they vanished into the deeper shadows.

Okay, Dylan. Think. His hands were shaking. Grieving people sometimes saw things, right? But no. He knew what he saw at the cemetery and what he saw now. This was real.

Someone was watching him. Someone who moved like they knew these grounds, who could appear and disappear at will. Someone who had reason to be interested in his arrival.

But why? What did they want?

He cased the gazebo again, this time looking for answers. Hidden behind ivy and wisteria was a low stone wall—no, a short stairwell, partially covered by aggressive vines. The top few steps disappeared into darkness.

What was down there?

He crouched beside the hidden stairs. A faint scent drifted up, not mildew, but something floral. Candle wax, maybe, or perfume.

Someone had been down there recently. His pulse quickened. *What did you hide down there, Mom? What were you so afraid of?*

Another twig snapped in the distance, louder this time.

They were getting careless. Or maybe they wanted him to know they're watching.

Dylan sprang to his feet, scanning the tree line. Nothing visible, but the gaze of unseen eyes pressed against his back like a physical touch.

Didn't look like they were trying to hurt him. Not yet. They were waiting for something. But what?

He didn't run, but he didn't linger either. Though there was still a hint of golden light, shadows were already creeping in. Whatever was down there could wait for morning—he wasn't about to risk missing something important in the fading light.

As he walked back toward the main house, he shook the tension from his shoulders. Mom and Dad were happy here once. The carved initials proved his parents had found love at Mirror Estate. But something else was lurking in the shadows, something that might explain why his mother spent twenty-five years running.

Mirror Estate was beautiful. Full of memories and secrets. But not everything here wanted to be seen.

As he glanced back one final time, the gardens lay peaceful in the dying light, giving no hint of their mysteries.

And now, someone was watching him. Someone who knew why he was here, maybe even what he was looking for.

CHAPTER 12
LEGACY AND DOUBTS

The library had always been Carol's favorite room in the house. It wasn't the largest, but it was the most peaceful. High shelves lined the walls, filled with volumes collected over generations—first-edition classics, business publications spanning decades, multiple translations of the Bible, and family favorites that had been read and reread.

A fire crackled in the hearth, more for ambiance than warmth. Afternoon light filtered through the tall windows, casting golden shafts across the Persian rug. The scent of old paper and aged wood added a comforting solemnity. Here, things didn't change unless you allowed them to.

She sat in the high-backed armchair near the window, sipping from a delicate crystal glass. Water, not wine. Too much to think about.

Next to her, Charles stood by one of the windows, a tumbler of scotch in hand. His tie was loosened, his usual crispness softened in the privacy of this room. But his eyes remained sharp as ever, following the figure moving beyond the glass.

Dylan.

"He's more like her than I expected." Carol put her glass on the windowsill and watched the boy—no, the man—meander down the gravel garden path. He stopped near the roses, hand brushing a vine like he was unsure if it was real.

"Same eyes." Charles nursed his scotch. "And he walks like her, as if the world has been made to include him. And he's just as curious as she was, checking out everything around him."

"He's young. And grieving."

He turned from the window, studying her over the rim of his glass. "Grief doesn't always bring people closer to family."

Carol let the remark settle and picked up her glass again. She had learned long ago not to rise to every challenge. She swirled the ice in her glass. "I didn't bring him here to trap him. I brought him here because he belongs. Even if he doesn't know it yet."

"Does he?"

She raised a brow.

"Belong?" he clarified. "You're talking about folding him into the family. Giving him a place. A future. But he didn't grow up in this world, Carol. You know that better than anyone."

She stood and leaned toward the window, careful not to spill her drink. Outside, Dylan had paused at the old fountain, fingers tracing the stone rim. The garden framed him in light and shadow, like a painting she couldn't stop staring at.

"He's her son. That should mean something."

"It does to you. Maybe even to me. But to the rest of the world, especially those with money on the line, he's a variable we haven't tested."

She pivoted. "You mean the board."

"I mean people with long memories and short patience. They remember how Maggie left. And they're not eager to bet the future on someone who just arrived."

She pressed her lips together. "The board members will come around. Most of them, anyway. They know he's the only living heir. There's no alternative."

Charles set his tumbler down. "You control seventy percent of M&M. The board members collectively hold twenty percent of the remaining shares. But that twenty percent includes some very vocal opponents who've never been comfortable with outsiders joining the family business. They're old-school traditionalists who believe leadership should come from within the established circle."

She ducked her head. That had been Ralph's wish, but…

"And don't forget about Maggie's disappearance."

"What about it? That was decades ago."

"It reinforced their belief that this family can't be trusted with leadership." He drew in a slow breath. "If they band together and create enough resistance, they could make Dylan's transition very difficult. Bad publicity, challenging his qualifications, questioning his commitment to the company."

A familiar tightness constricted her chest. "What do you suggest?"

"Gradual introduction. Let him prove himself in smaller roles before announcing any succession plans. Give the board time to see his potential rather than just his inexperience."

"And if some of them refuse to accept him, regardless?"

Charles fell quiet. Then he raised his glass as if in salute. "We'll deal with that when it happens. You still hold the controlling interest. But a divided board could hurt the company's value, especially if the conflict becomes public."

She said nothing. Her gaze followed Dylan as he wandered farther into the garden, disappearing behind the ivy curtain draping the gazebo.

"I don't doubt your intentions, Carol. But I question whether he'll want this responsibility. At least right now."

"He came. That counts for something."

"Yes. But some men come for belonging. Some come for opportunity." He kept his tone even. "And some come for the payout and then walk away."

Carol's fingers tightened around the stem of her glass.

"I'm not saying he will," he added. "But this place, this life… It's a lot to take in. Especially for someone who's never had it."

She exhaled. "Then he'll have to learn. I'd rather give him the chance to grow into it than shut him out before he's begun."

He studied her face. "Just be careful. Ralph and you built something worth protecting. Don't give your heart to the idea of a legacy before you know the man who might inherit it."

She faced the window again. Dylan was out of sight now. The leaves shifted in the breeze, but nothing moved in the clearing. "I know what I'm doing. I just don't know if I have the time to wait."

Outside, Dylan reappeared from behind the gazebo and stood still, scanning the trees. His body language had shifted. Not afraid, but alert.

Her gaze narrowed as her grandson stood motionless, tense. "What's he looking at?"

Charles closed in on the window too. "Something spooked him. Could be anything, a squirrel, a bird."

She resettled deep in her chair. "He's jumpy. I suppose grief affects people differently."

He drained the rest of his drink and set the glass on a coaster. "You're betting a lot on him."

"I have little left to bet with. And no one else to bet on."

He picked up his briefcase. "I'll keep an eye on things."

"I know."

He hesitated at the threshold. "Carol, what if he decides he doesn't want any of this? What if he's not capable of handling it?"

Beyond the window, the garden stood empty, Dylan having disappeared from view. The fountain still gurgled, the breeze rustled the roses, and the light kept shifting across the lawn.

She didn't want to think about that possibility. Couldn't afford to.

CHAPTER 13

THREATS AND OFFERS

Dylan followed the stone pathway back to the main house; the afternoon sun angled lower now, casting elongated shadows through the trees. He paused near the edge to glance down the row of trees toward the Mirror Estate sign carved in stone.

Nothing moved. No people. No sound. Still, that prickling feeling returned, like someone had been watching and vanished the second he looked.

Strange. He shook his head clear.

As he resumed walking, he slowed by something he'd missed earlier; a smaller, older sign affixed to a stone pillar near the house, carved deep with elegant serif letters.

Agnes House. So the main house had a name. Did the guesthouse have one too?

At the front steps, he rang the doorbell and waited. Seconds passed before the door opened.

"Oh, hello. I didn't know you left." Max stepped back to let him in.

"Sean took me through the tunnel to the restaurant."

Max offered a knowing smile. "Be careful. You may not fit in your clothes after a week."

Dylan laughed. "I know. Maybe I ought to hit the gym."

"We have one on this floor. Sean loves to play with that fancy equipment. Would you like me to take you there?"

"Not now, thanks. I'll check it out later. I'd like to see if Carol has time to chat."

Max nodded. "She's in the library. I'll let her know you're looking for her."

Dylan thanked him and headed toward the stairs. The house was quiet again, as if it had absorbed the noise and warmth from earlier and stored it somewhere out of reach.

Back in his room, he considered calling Tommy, but his friend would still be at work. His duffel bag was where he'd left it, half zipped on the floor. He picked it up and dropped it inside the walk-in closet.

In the en suite bathroom, he splashed water on his face, and the coolness chased away the tension still clinging to him. The towels were plush. The marble countertop gleamed. A whirlpool tub sat like a throne beneath the tall window. Such luxury felt unreal.

He stepped out into the bedroom again, toweling off his hands, and stopped at something on the floor. A folded piece of paper lay inside the door.

He hadn't heard a knock. Maybe the water muffled it.

He crouched, picked it up, and unfolded it. No name. Just a single sentence typed in all caps:

YOU DON'T BELONG HERE. GO HOME.

How ridiculous. Who did something like that? He crumpled the message, but even as he tried to dismiss it, his heart thudded. He spread the paper back out. Some kind of prank, maybe. Someone trying to mess with the new guy.

But the more he looked at the stark black letters, the less like a prank it felt. The watcher in the gardens. The figure at the cemetery. The constant feeling of being observed.

Someone really didn't want him here. His hands began to shake. This wasn't paranoia. Someone was trying to scare him away.

He opened the door and checked up and down the hallway. Nothing. No shadows. No sound. Whoever left this vanished as completely as the figure in the gardens.

He shivered.

Who even had access to his room? Max? One of the staff? Carol?

He hated suspecting Carol. She invited him here, after all. But someone here didn't want him around. Someone with keys, someone who could move through the house undetected.

Heat built in his chest, even as shivers coursed over his spine. "I have every right to be here," he whispered, his hands clenching. "This is *my* family."

But the chill seeped in deeper, overcoming the anger. If someone was willing to slip threatening notes under his door, what else might they be willing to do?

Someone knocked. He'd left the door ajar while studying the hallway.

He pulled it open with more force than necessary, half expecting to catch the note-leaver.

Instead, Carol jolted back a step, her eyes wide.

"Oh, hi." He folded the note and slipped it into his pocket.

"Sean told me he gave you the grand tour. I was hoping you might have time to visit with your grandmother?"

"Of course." He stepped aside. Should he tell her about the note? Or would he sound paranoid? "You want to come in?"

"Let's go down to the kitchen. More comfortable there."

"Okay." He followed her downstairs. "Sean took me to the restaurant. Lorraine's cooking is incredible."

"It wasn't always a restaurant. When Connor and Lorraine wanted to open a restaurant and were looking for a place, I offered to let them use the space. I've always known she could cook, and the timing worked out for everyone."

She led him to a cozy dining area.

Max appeared with a tray of tea and delicate cookies arranged on fine china, then asked, "Would you like coffee instead?"

"Decaf, if you have it, please. And sweetener."

Max returned shortly with a carafe, sweetener packets, and creamer. He placed them on the table with quiet precision, then disappeared again.

Carol poured her tea, then settled in, and her light-brown eyes seemed to see right through him. "So, tell me about Maggie."

"Oh. She went by Mimi."

"She was always Maggie here." Her smile dimmed. "I heard it was breast cancer."

The familiar tightness returned to his chest. "She waited too long to see the doctor. She didn't like these medical appointments. By the time they confirmed the diagnosis..." He swallowed, steadying his voice. "It was stage four. Inoperable."

"How long did she have?"

"She was diagnosed just over two years ago. They tried some treatments, and she responded quite well; stabilized for a little while. But a year ago, things started going downhill fast. She chose to enter hospice several weeks ago. Her faith sustained her through it all. Our parish priest came every week to bring her Communion, and she received the Last Sacraments."

He managed a small smile. "She said she wasn't afraid because she knew where she was going."

Carol's hands trembled around her teacup. "She always had such strong faith. Even as a little girl, she'd insist on saying grace at every meal and praying before bed."

They sat in silence; the loss settling between them.

"Do you know why she left?" Dylan finished his coffee. "I mean, I grew up thinking her whole family was gone. That she was all alone in the world."

She let out a slow breath, the creamy silk blouse seeming to deflate. "I don't blame her for keeping us a secret. I'm sure she believed it was for your protection. And she might have been right. Ralph, your grandfather, passed about two years ago. I had hoped she would come home then, but she didn't."

"Maybe she wanted to, but by then, the cancer had already started. She was probably too sick to think about traveling, though she never let on how bad it was getting."

"Perhaps." Carol's voice carried decades of regret. "There's so much I wish I had asked her myself." She smoothed back her too-shiny brown hair, seeming to shake herself from the melancholy. A gentleness softened her features. "But let's talk about you. What have you been doing since college? Charles had his investigators look into your background, so I've read the basics. But I'd like to hear it from you."

Dylan gave her the same summary he'd shared with his boss, only he included his current role as a management trainee, his hope for a permanent offer, and his rotations through various departments.

She listened with genuine interest. "Very good. If I understand correctly, you've worked in leasing, accounting, and development. Is there one area that particularly appealed to you?"

"Asset management or development."

She tilted her head. "Any interest in hospitality or hotel management? It's not so different from what you've done. Still sales, budgeting, property improvements, but with guests instead of tenants."

Dylan narrowed his eyes. "I suppose I'm open to it, but why do you ask?"

"Because that's a good starting point. I'm sure we can find a perfect fit for you at Marino and Marino."

He blinked. "Marino and Marino, as in M&M Enterprises?"

She nodded as if it were the most natural thing in the world. "Your great-grandfather and grandfather started it. We still call it that, even though Ralph has been gone for two years."

"I thought I read something about import and export?"

"They got out of that decades ago. Today, our primary focus is in the hospitality industry, though we do have interests in commercial real estate." She folded her hands in her lap, fiddling with her wedding band. "I don't attend board meetings in person anymore, but I participate virtually when important decisions need to be made. When you're ready, Charles can give you a proper tour and introduce you to the department heads."

"But... but I don't understand." He sat back in his chair. He hadn't even unpacked his bag, and now she was talking about giving him a place in the family business. "Are you offering me a job?"

"I'm offering you your birthright." She raised her chin. "There's a board meeting next Tuesday. I'd like you to attend as an observer, just to get a feel for how we operate. And we should set up meetings with the various department heads so you can see where your interests lie."

The note in his pocket seemed to grow heavier. Someone wanted him gone, but Carol was planning his entire future.

"I... I'll need to think about it."

Her smile faltered. "Of course. It's a lot to process all at once."

Max returned with impeccable timing, placing a second tray on the sideboard. "Time for your medication, Ms. Carol."

Dylan sat back in his chair, the words *Marino and Marino* still echoing in his mind. The threatening note. The job offer. The watcher in the gardens.

He came to find answers. Now he'd been handed a future he hadn't asked for, and someone else was trying to scare him away from it.

What had he gotten himself into?

CHAPTER 14

VOICES IN THE DARK

By 8 p.m., Dylan couldn't stand the silence anymore. The estate felt too quiet, too watchful, and the conversation with Carol about his birthright only made things worse. He grabbed his laptop and headed to the balcony, where the fading summer light cast a dim golden glow across the grounds.

Maybe talking to Tommy would help clear his head.

The gardens stretched before him in amber hues, formal hedges and ancient oaks creating long shadows across the manicured lawn. In Seattle, Tommy would just be getting off work—perfect timing.

"This is unbelievable!" Dylan said into the camera, trying to inject some enthusiasm into his voice. The balcony offered the perfect backdrop. He could show off the view while escaping the feeling that the walls themselves were listening.

"Oh, man, M&M Enterprises. Wow. You better not forget little old me."

"She didn't exactly offer me anything." His fingers drummed against the laptop. He forced them still, a nervous habit his mother had tried to correct.

"But she's going to. Why else would she find you? She's old. You're the heir she's looking for."

"This is just... too much." He stood, unable to sit still. The tension in his shoulders had been building all evening, radiating up his neck like a vise.

"Wow, nice view. Pan around so I can see better. Hey, don't stop."

But Dylan had stopped rotating the laptop, his free hand fumbling in his pocket. The note might as well have been burning his fingers. He pulled it out and held it up to the screen, his hand trembling slightly.

Tommy leaned closer to his camera. "What's that?"

"This was on the floor when I came out of the bathroom." Dylan's voice came out hoarser than he'd intended. "Earlier today."

Tommy's expression shifted. "That's creepy. Wait. Was this before or after your grandma offered you the kingdom?"

"Nobody offered me anything." Dylan moved to scan the tree line. Even in the golden evening light, the spaces between the oaks looked impenetrable. "But it was before our conversation."

"Oh. Then maybe someone doesn't want you here. You know, upsetting the apple cart. Maybe someone else expected to inherit, and then, bam! You show up. In lots of crime shows, that's a motive for murder."

His pulse jumped. "Please don't tell me someone is plotting to kill me."

"What? You have that look."

"Well..." Dylan rubbed the back of his neck where the tension had settled. He hadn't voiced it, not even to himself. "I have this feeling I'm being watched. Like someone's spying on me."

He faced the grounds again, his shoulder blades prickling. The sensation of unseen eyes crawled across his skin like ice water. The formal gardens lay quiet under the soft pools of landscape lighting, but beyond them, where Spanish moss draped the trees in darkness, anything could be lurking.

"There you go. I'd hire a bodyguard if I were you.'

"I have enough stress as it is. You don't need to make me more nervous. I just want to meet my mom's family, not tack a target on my back." Dylan's gaze kept returning to the dark spaces between the trees.

"Dude, news flash, the rich and famous always have targets on their backs. Hey, my bus is here. Gotta go. Stay safe."

"Yeah, thanks."

He closed the laptop and remained still, watching the last daylight fade. His heart hammered against his ribs in the quiet.

Was it paranoia? Or instinct?

Someone didn't want him here. Now, he was starting to wonder why.

By midnight, he gave up on sleep. He'd been pacing between the king-size bed and the balcony doors for hours, checking the lock repeatedly. Every time he closed his eyes, he saw that folded note, felt unseen eyes watching from the darkness.

Outside, the Florida night whispered with unfamiliar sounds, palm fronds rustling, the distant splash of something in the pond, an owl's haunting call. So different from his Seattle apartment, where sirens and late-night arguments from the hallway had been his lullaby. Here, the silence hung heavy, expectant.

Watching.

When exhaustion claimed him around four in the morning, his sleep was fractured, full of whispers and shadows.

"Dylan, can you hear me?"

His eyes snapped open. The voice seemed to drift from the air-conditioning vent, soft as a sigh.

His pulse thundered in his ears. This wasn't real. Grief could make you hear things. Tommy had mentioned that after his grandfather died.

He listened to the silence, counting his breaths. Just a dream. Just stress.

"Remember what I told you?"

The key around his neck warmed against his skin. He sat up, the silk sheets pooling around his waist, and pressed his palm against the slight weight through his shirt.

Of course he remembered. But he still didn't know what the key was for. And what secrets?

Oh, Mom. Why couldn't you have stayed awake long enough to explain?

"Find it. Then you need to leave."

This was too much. He dropped to his knees beside the bed, pressing his elbows into the mattress and burying his face in his hands. He pictured her, kneeling, calm, sure. He couldn't manage that. He couldn't even breathe right.

"Just... take it," he muttered. "Take something. Anything." He didn't know if he was talking to God or losing his grip.

But instead of his mother's peace, the voice came again, urgent now: *"Find it. It's not safe. Hurry, find it."*

His brow furrowed. The voice seemed to come from everywhere and nowhere—the walls, the ceiling, his own fractured mind.

"Mom? Is that you?" He was talking to himself. Great. Now he was hearing voices.

"Find it. It's not safe. Hurry, find it."

He stood up and rubbed his face with both hands. This house was making him crazy.

Still, he remembered her hand closing around his; the key pressed into his palm, her voice thick with medication and urgency. The words had sounded like nonsense, but they haunted him now.

He couldn't leave. Not yet.

He needed to know what the key opened. What secrets his mother meant. And what Carol wanted from him.

Too many questions, and no way to answer them at four in the morning.

Three hours later, his neck might as well have been twisted in a vise, and a dull headache pulsed behind his eyes. Dylan rubbed his temples as he made his way to the kitchen, where Max was already preparing for the day.

"Good morning." Dylan tried to keep the exhaustion from his voice. "Do you know everyone who works here? And at the restaurant?"

Max stilled at the counter, not at all subtle about taking in the dark circles under Dylan's eyes. "Yes, and no. I know all the household employees. We use a cleaning service, so I don't know those folks. You'll need to ask Lorraine about the restaurant workers. Anyone in particular you're looking for?"

"Not really. Just curious, is all." Dylan kept his tone light, but he was thinking of the note. The voice. The unease that settled in his chest. His fingers started drumming against the counter—that old nervous habit—and he forced them still.

"You've met Duke, our chauffeur and handyman," Max added. "Solid guy. Been with us a long time."

"Right." Dylan nodded toward the counter. "Do you mind if I make a waffle? I saw the waffle iron earlier."

"Of course. We have batter ready in the fridge." Max pulled out a container and handed it to him. "And this." He offered a can of cooking spray from a lower cabinet.

"Thanks." Dylan plugged in the iron and started prepping, grateful for something to do with his hands. "Sounds like you've been here a long time."

"Since before Mr. Ralph married Ms. Carol. Was here back when she was just the young lady who came to visit."

Dylan froze, distracted from his anxiety. "So... you knew my mother?"

"I did."

"Will you tell me about her?" Hope pitched his voice too

high. He cleared his throat and tempered his tone. "Any stories?"

Max's expression softened. "She was a good little girl. But I didn't know her well. Abby was her nanny. She left when your mother went off to boarding school." Max paused, seeming to search for something in his memory. "Whenever Ms. Maggie came back here, she spent most of her time with the kids at the old orphanage."

Dylan blinked, his tension forgotten. "Orphanage? I didn't know there was one around here."

"Oh, it closed years ago. The chapel is still there. It's since grown into a parish church, Holy Angels, but we still call it a chapel. All the nuns have passed on or are in nursing homes. Fr. Phil is still the pastor, though."

An orphanage. Dylan's chest tightened. His mother, surrounded by wealth and privilege, had chosen to spend her time with children who had nothing. How like the woman who'd raised him, always putting others first, always finding those who needed help.

"I assume the priest knew my mother?"

"Oh yes." Max resumed preparing breakfast. "She was there so much, Mr. Ralph thought she wanted to be a nun. He wasn't a religious man, and he wanted an heir. Ms. Carol, though, was glad."

That might explain everything. Her faith. Her quiet strength. Her secrets. The way she'd knelt by her bed each night, surrendering her worries to something larger than herself.

"Where's this chapel?"

"It's close by." Max gave him directions, his voice fading into background noise.

Dylan repeated the route silently, already picturing the place. As he did, he rubbed the tight muscles at the base of his neck. His mother had found peace in places of worship, surrounded by those who needed help. She'd always carried that serenity with her, even in their cramped apartment.

Maybe at the chapel, he could find some of that same peace. Maybe there, among the echoes of his mother's prayers, the answers would come.

And maybe the voice in his head would still.

The key around his neck seemed to pulse with his anticipation. Whatever secrets his mother had died protecting, whatever truth lay buried in her past, it was time to uncover it.

Holy Angels Chapel was waiting.

CHAPTER 15

THE MESSAGE

Halfway up the stairs, his mind already racing toward Holy Angels Chapel and the answers it might hold, Dylan saw her.

A woman slipped out of his room with fluid, practiced movements. She moved as if she knew where every creaking floorboard lay.

"Hey!" he called, his voice echoing in the hallway.

No answer.

He hustled down the hall, adrenaline shot through him. In that fleeting moment, the familiar turn of her head, the way she held her shoulders, she could've been his mother. Not the frail woman ravaged by cancer, but his mother from years ago. Healthy. Whole.

But that was impossible. Wasn't it?

A ghost? His mind rejected the thought, but his chest tightened with hope and something deeper, grief so raw it made him dizzy.

The woman shifted toward him and smiled, her lips moving.

His breath caught. She was mouthing his name.

"Mom," he whispered, already moving faster.

"Hello, Dylan."

Townsend's voice cut through like a blade.

Dylan stopped.

The attorney stepped out of a room to the left.

When Dylan turned back, she was gone.

"Hi." Dylan pointed down the hall where he'd seen the woman. "Did you see... a woman? She was just right there."

Townsend followed his line of sight. "I saw no one when I opened the door. Just you." He gestured down the corridor. "That hallway leads nowhere. Just the window at the end."

Sure enough, the hallway ended in a large sunlit window with no adjoining doorways. Unless she'd ducked into a side room... if she'd even been there at all.

Was he losing his mind?

He tapped his temple once to shake off the absurd thought. "Right. Sorry, I..."

Townsend frowned, his focus narrowing in on Dylan's face. "I arrived early to check on things for Carol. She asked me to speak with you about some practical matters, such as your mother's estate and your current financial situation. She's worried you might be struggling after the funeral expenses."

He shifted. "I'm managing."

"I'm sure. But Carol would like to help. Transfer some funds to cover any immediate needs, handle the paperwork to settle your mother's affairs properly." Townsend held up a hand, remaining gentle but professional. "No strings attached. Just family taking care of family."

Dylan nodded, but his thoughts kept circling back to the woman in the hallway. "I... I appreciate that. But I have to ask— I thought I saw her just now. My mom. Obviously, that can't be. Just... my imagination, right?"

Townsend's expression shifted. Something flickered behind his eyes, a flash of recognition suppressed. His jaw tightened almost as if the man knew more than he was willing to say.

"You must miss her. That's understandable." Townsend's gaze lingered on Dylan's face, searching. "Grief can... play tricks on the mind."

Although the lawyer's tone remained measured, something lingered underneath, concern, maybe even worry. As if the lawyer knew what Dylan had seen, and it wasn't a grief-induced hallucination.

"Is everything all right?" Dylan asked at the subtle change in the man's demeanor.

"Yes." Townsend's mask slipped back into place. "Just... if you see anything else unusual, anything at all, perhaps you should mention it to Carol. Or to me."

The unspoken warning made Dylan's skin prickle.

What was happening to him? First the threatening note, then voices in his dreams, and now seeing his dead mother in broad daylight. Maybe grief *could* break a person's mind. Maybe the stress was overwhelming him.

He shook his head. "I appreciate the offer about the finances. Can we talk about it later? I need to think."

"Of course. Take all the time you need."

As soon as Townsend returned to the guest room, Dylan strode outside. He needed answers; about the key, about his mother's secrets, and about whether he was losing his grip on reality.

According to Max, Holy Angels was half a mile from the estate if he took the path to the left after exiting the property. He could have asked Duke for a ride, but he chose to walk. He needed the air.

But once he passed the property gate, the hairs on the back of his neck rose again. He paused. Still no one visible, but the feeling persisted, those unseen eyes following his every move.

Maybe he was just jumpy. Maybe this place, this estate with its whispers and shadows, was getting to him.

He pressed on, inhaling the cool breeze that drifted from the estate's pond. It smelled fresh and clean, like cut grass, water, and stone. The path curved through the woods and cleared again near a cluster of aged brick, whitewashed fences, and a wrought iron sign for Holy Angels Chapel.

He stopped at the gates, where a metal plaque listed Mass times and the names of past donors. Beyond the chapel stood the crumbling remains of what had once been St. Agnes Orphanage—brick buildings with boarded windows, their white-washed walls faded and peeling. Vines had reclaimed the structures, wrapping around broken gutters and creeping through foundation cracks.

The stone chapel itself remained well maintained. With its arched windows gleaming in the morning sun and the peaked roof intact, it stood like a faithful guardian beside the abandoned orphanage, the only part of the old complex still serving its original purpose.

He gripped the iron handles of the heavy oak double doors. They gave way, unlocked, and he stepped into cool and quiet. Dusty sunlight streamed through stained glass, coloring the wooden pews in patches of red, blue, and gold. Older women knelt toward the front, praying the rosary aloud in soft, steady voices. The familiar rhythm reminded him of his mother, and fresh grief tightened his chest.

"May I help you?"

A priest in a light-gray shirt and a clerical collar approached from a side aisle. Probably in his early sixties, he carried himself well, but his graying hair and something unspoken made him seem older. When their eyes met, the priest stopped midstride, his weathered face draining of color.

"Hi." Dylan smiled. "Are you Fr. Phil?"

"Yes." The priest blinked, then gawked as if Dylan were

someone he'd been waiting decades to see again. Fr. Phil's breath caught. "You look exactly like him."

Dylan's eyebrows rose. "Like who?"

"Your father. Mickey." His voice carried decades of memory and something that might have been regret. "I've been expecting you, son."

The priest motioned toward a side aisle. "There's something for you. From your mother."

CHAPTER 16

FAMILY SECRETS

The scent hit Dylan before anything else—incense and old wood and something that reminded him of his mother's prayer book. He followed Fr. Phil down the narrow hallway, his footsteps whispering on creaking floorboards that must've supported decades of confessions and conversations like this one.

The priest led him to an office tucked behind the sacristy. A crucifix hung on the wall above a modest bookshelf filled with worn theological texts and what looked like donated paperbacks. This was no lavish clergy suite, just a quiet, worn-in space.

When Fr. Phil gestured to a chair across from his desk, Dylan sat, still unsure what to expect.

The priest booted up his desktop computer, his fingers typing with quiet efficiency. The clicking of keys intruded in the silence.

"I'm forwarding an email to you." Fr. Phil paused typing. "What's your email address?"

Dylan gave it. Seconds later, his phone buzzed with a new message.

The priest sat back. "Before you read it, let me explain. After she left, I didn't see your mother for years. Then, out of nowhere, this email showed up. Her instructions were clear. This is meant for you and only you."

Dylan lowered his phone. "When did it arrive?"

"Just the other day. Right after I found out you were coming to the estate."

That made Dylan pause. His finger hovered over his phone screen as he unlocked it and opened the forwarded email with an attachment.

He skimmed the headers, Fr. Phil to him. Then, an unknown email address to Fr. Phil with the message:

> *Phil,*
> *Please give this to Dylan, no one else. I believe you already know*
> *he's Mickey's and my son. ONLY Dylan, please.*
> *Thank you!*
> *Signed, Maggie*

He didn't tap the video attachment. Not yet.

His chest tightened at her signature, her asking Fr. Phil to take care of him one last time. He scrolled back up to the forwarded header. Frank Rogers, the gruff attorney from the funeral.

"She wasn't that tech savvy. She must've asked this lawyer to help her send this. He gave me his card at the funeral." *Why didn't you tell me, Mom?*

Fr. Phil nodded. "A scheduled delivery. That makes sense. Still, part of me wondered if the story of her death had been a mistake. Wishful thinking, I guess."

Dylan looked at him. "Sorry."

The priest waved it off. "You don't need to apologize. It's just... strange. To hear from someone after they're gone."

"Yeah." His throat felt tight. "It is."

How long had she been preparing for her death? What other arrangements had she made that he didn't know about?

He pocketed his phone and leaned back in the chair. "If you've got time... I'd like to know more about her. About what happened back then."

"I have some time now. And I'm glad to tell you what I know." The priest shut down his computer and rolled his chair to face Dylan fully. "I met your mother when I was here as a transitional deacon—I'd returned after my ordination. Your father was preparing to graduate, and your mother was home for the summer, just before her senior year if I recall correctly."

"They met here? On the estate?"

"Yes. I knew both of them. Your father helped out around the chapel. Fr. Bob, my predecessor, had him handle the computer systems back when very few people knew how. Your mother... Well, she was usually nearby." The priest chuckled. "She had a way of making herself invisible when she wanted to."

A small smile pulled at Dylan's lips. "She used to do that. Disappear into a crowd. Or blend in at the back of a room."

"I mostly saw her during holidays. You know she went to boarding school, right? Anyway, I remember her slipping into the chapel late at night to sit and sketch. One time, she left a pencil drawing of the stained glass window in the hymnal rack. It was good. Clean lines, beautiful shading. She saw things most people missed."

"She always had a good eye. She helped me set up my first dorm room. Made it feel like a home."

Fr. Phil stared at the cabinet to Dylan's left and appeared lost in thought. "She was clever. Let people think she was spending time here because of faith. But really... she was spending time with your father. Forbidden love, I suppose."

Dylan's eyebrows lifted. "Because of her family?"

"How much do you know about them?"

"Almost nothing. She told me they were all dead. Then, right before she passed, she said that wasn't true. But she never explained."

Fr. Phil drummed his fingers, like he was playing a piano. "The Marino family amassed their wealth generations ago through criminal means. Bootlegging. Gambling. Bribes."

The words hung in the air like smoke. Dylan's first instinct was to shake his head. "That can't be right. Carol seems so... normal. Kind."

"Your great-grandfather was the first to try to sever ties with that legacy. Whether he succeeded... I'm not sure. Your grandfather tried as well. Your grandmother has never been part of it. In fact, she was instrumental in getting your grandfather to turn his life around. But some ties are hard to cut clean."

That explained why he didn't get any dangerous vibes from Carol. Or Max. If they were criminals, they were nothing like what he'd imagined.

But then what about the estate's security measures? The way conversations seemed carefully measured? The threatening note someone had slipped under his door? Maybe the criminal world hadn't let go of his family as easily as his family tried to let go of it.

"So my grandfather went legitimate?"

"He tried. Whether some ties are ever fully severed..." Fr. Phil shrugged.

Dylan leaned forward even as revulsion curled through him. Criminals didn't walk away from the life without repercussions. He had to have made some kind of deal with law enforcement. But what kind? And who else knew about it?

"I don't think your mother knew much about the family history when she was younger. But meeting your father... that may have changed things."

"She never told me anything," Dylan said. "Nothing about this. Nothing about him."

"Your father's father was a police officer. He died in the line of duty when Mickey was just fourteen. The only relative who could have taken him in—an elderly aunt—had suffered a stroke and couldn't care for herself, let alone a grieving teenager."

Dylan's chest tightened. No wonder his father understood what it was like to feel alone in the world. No wonder he'd fallen in love with someone else who felt trapped by circumstances beyond her control.

"So he came here?"

"Fr. Bob took him in. Mickey was brilliant with computers, even then. He helped modernize our systems. He went to college on a full scholarship. Software engineering or something like that. Last I heard, he had a good job in Atlanta."

Dylan's brows knotted. "You kept in touch with them?"

The priest blinked as if realizing too late what he'd revealed. "Well, let's say your father let me know his forwarding address."

Fr. Phil knew more than he was saying, but now might not be the time to press. Dylan changed tactics. "So even if my mother wasn't part of the family business, it didn't matter. She was still a Marino."

"And a Marino getting involved with someone connected to law enforcement, well, that wasn't the match her father would've chosen."

"Did they elope?" Dylan asked. "Was that the plan?"

Fr. Phil stared at the cabinet again. His fingers continued their desktop piano playing. Then he sighed, stood up, crossed the room, unlocked the cabinet's bottom drawer, and retrieved a box. He put the box on his desk, opened it, and fished out a photo. "You should have this."

Dylan's gaze stayed on the priest for a beat longer, searching his expression, trying to read behind the gesture. Only when the photo brushed his fingers did he take it, carefully, like it might crumble.

At first, it didn't register. Two people, dressed up, caught mid-laugh in the soft light of some long-ago afternoon. In a church.

Then, his breath caught.

He knew that smile. Knew those eyes.

The woman in a white dress was his mother—younger, radiant, aglow with happiness. And the man in a suit looked eerily like himself. This had to be his father. "Their wedding?"

Fr. Phil nodded.

A soft knock brushed the outer door, and a woman's voice mumbled something indistinct.

Dylan pocketed the photo and stood. "You've been very helpful, Father. Thank you for your time."

"We can talk more later, if you'd like."

"I'd like that."

He was already pulling out his phone as he left the office.

Back in the hallway, he opened the email again. His mother's message waited in his inbox like a time bomb.

> *Dylan,*
> *Please view the attached video files in private.*
> *Love,*
> *Mom*

The key around his neck felt heavier than ever. His mother's secrets, his father's death, the family's dark legacy. It was all connected somehow. And somewhere in that video message lay the truth that had gotten his father killed.

His thumb hovered over the attachment.

Soon. But first, he needed to find somewhere truly private. Because if his mother had gone to the trouble of scheduling this message through Frank Rogers, if she'd waited until after her death to reveal her secrets, then what she had to say was dangerous enough to get him killed too.

30 YEARS AGO

Mickey Roche's hands stilled on the keyboard as Maggie Marino stepped into Fr. Bob's office. Two months at boarding school had somehow made her even more polished, if that was possible. Her summer dress probably cost more than he'd see in a month, but it was the way she moved, like she belonged everywhere she went, that reminded him why he'd been avoiding her letters.

Some things were better left alone.

"Something on my face?" Frowning, she settled into the visitor's chair like she planned to stay.

"Oh no. Just thinking." He turned back to the computer installation, focusing on the cables and connections. The ancient priest was kind and friendly, but he belonged to the old school. When Mickey had tried to explain how a modem worked, Fr. Bob had all but thought it was voodoo.

Mrs. Marino had offered to donate a top-of-the-line computer system to the orphanage, but the priest had asked if she would donate cash instead, money for the children, not gadgets. She'd written the check, then sent the computers anyway in classic Marino behavior. Generous, but on their terms. Always on their terms.

Did Maggie know how her family operated? Or was she just as controlled as everyone else in their orbit?

"You didn't write like you promised." She scooted her chair closer, and he caught the scent of her expensive shampoo. "I told you everything about the happenings at boarding school, and you didn't tell me anything about the orphanage."

"I did write."

"Yeah, two letters in the whole two months." Hurt lurked beneath that accusation. "I told you everything, about the girls, the classes, how much I missed..." She stopped herself.

"Missed what?" His fingers stilled on the cables.

"You know what."

He shrugged, not trusting himself to meet her eyes. "What's there to tell? There's no weekend outings or joint school events."

"I wish Daddy would let me go to a local school so we could do things together. We could go to Orlando all the time. You know, Disney World."

Mickey kept his focus on the computer. Disney World. Like it was nothing. Like dropping fifty bucks on a day trip was something everyone did on weekends.

"You have your life. I have mine." He plugged the last cord in with more vigor than necessary.

The words also came out harder than he intended. She'd never understand what it was like to count every dollar, to know college was his only shot at something better. Her father expected her to marry someone from their world; someone with a trust fund and family connections, not a cop's orphaned kid with nothing but good grades and borrowed clothes.

She got up and came around to stand next to him. "I thought we were friends. I thought you liked me."

The problem was he did like her. More than liked her. But

liking Maggie Marino was like admiring a painting in a museum —you could look, but you'd never take it home.

"We are friends." He forced himself to meet her eyes. "But you're going back to school in a few weeks. And I'm staying here."

"That doesn't mean—"

"It means exactly that." He turned back to the computer, fingers working the connections. "Your father has plans for you. College, probably somewhere prestigious. Maybe Europe. The kind of life I'll never be part of."

"Maggie, so good to see you." Fr. Bob's voice boomed from just outside the office, cutting through the tension. "Let me introduce you to Deacon Phil. He'll be ordained next year, but he'll be here to help and be my assistant."

Mickey's shoulders relaxed. Saved by the priest, again.

"I'm sorry. I should have been here."

Mickey shrugged at Phil's words as they walked across the orphanage grounds. "Not your fault. You have a higher calling." The summer evenings were always nicer and cooler than the afternoons, and the cicadas were beginning their symphony. "Did you ask to come here?"

"You don't ask for a placement. I mentioned it to one of the priests. Turns out, he's got a lot of pull in the assignment department. He got me here."

"That's good."

"Mickey, I can be your guardian. I could hold off on ordination."

"No." Mickey pushed every bit of his will into that one word. "I mean, if you don't want to be a priest, that's cool. Just don't do it on my account. I'm happy here."

"But aren't you almost seventeen? You'll age out of the

system before you graduate? You have two more years of school."

"No worries. Fr. Bob said I could stay until I graduate. In fact, I can stay until I'm ready to be on my own. But I wouldn't do that. I'm dirt poor, so I'll get free money to go to college."

Phil chuckled. "I guess you're right. Engineering?"

"Maybe software development. I don't know yet."

They continued walking in silence, passing the garden the nuns maintained. Fireflies blinked in the gathering dusk, and somewhere in the distance, soft voices called the younger children in for evening prayers.

"Are you dating Maggie, the girl back there?"

Mickey's step didn't falter, but something tightened in his chest. "We're friends. She'll go back to boarding school in the fall."

"That's not what I asked."

They walked past a weathered statue of St. Francis, its surface worn smooth by years of Florida rain and humidity. "Her father would never approve of someone like me."

"Someone like you?"

"Someone with no family, no money, no connections." No self-pity, just facts. "I've seen how Mr. Marino looks at people. He's polite to Fr. Bob because he has to be, but he measures everyone by what they can offer his family. I'm not prime son-in-law material."

"Maybe she doesn't care what her father thinks."

Mickey laughed, but no humor accompanied it. "She's gonna be seventeen and lives in a mansion. She cares."

Phil fell quiet, then seemed to remember something. "I hope you didn't tell anyone about us."

"No. Nobody's business."

"Good. Let's keep it that way."

As they headed back toward the main building, light still

glowed in Fr. Bob's office windows. Maggie was probably still there, probably wondering why he'd been so cold earlier.

Maybe it was better this way. Maybe keeping his distance now would save them both from complications later.

But it was already too late for that, wasn't it? At least for himself.

CHAPTER 17
HIDDEN MESSAGES

Dylan's fingers trembled as he clutched his phone outside Holy Angels Chapel. Where could he watch the video his mother sent without being seen?

He could find a tree somewhere, but his phone screen was too tiny. Besides, the glare made it hard to see outside without a cover. With sighting that woman and the threatening note, he ruled out the main house, but where else? Lorraine's Kitchen wouldn't be private enough.

Yes, the tour. Sean would show him a private place.

When he neared the estate, he pressed the gate's call button, and whoever was manning the camera opened the gate for him. Inside, he scanned the surroundings. Why did he always feel like he was being watched? Was he? Or was he getting paranoid?

Sean came running. "Hey, Dylan. I've been looking all over for you. Ready for your grand tour?"

"Just what I've been hoping for. Let me get a drink first."

The Mirror Estate covered several acres. Sean had a future as a tour guide, giving excellent commentary about each room and building.

As they walked alongside the pond, Dylan nudged a pebble with his shoe. "Hey, if I want to read something in peace, where should I go so no one will disturb me? Not inside the house, I'd rather be out getting some fresh air."

Sean studied him. "You're too tall for my hideout. Hmm... I know. Here." He grabbed Dylan's hand and hauled him forward.

Rather than take him to some secluded place, the boy led him to the gazebo by the pond, out in the open.

Sean pulled him down to sit on the bench. "Perfect."

"How can this be private?"

"Nobody comes here. If you sit down, nobody can see you from the house."

"I remember noticing the gazebo from the balcony in my room." But he hadn't been close enough to discern anything. And under this roof, he could see the phone screen better. Being out in the open would let him see when someone was coming.

"This will do. Thanks." He clamped a hand on the boy's shoulder. "You're the only kid I see around here. Don't you hang out with friends?"

A big grin bunched up the boy's cheeks. "I start summer camp next week. Swimming, soccer, football, basketball. A different theme each week. And this year, I get to do rock climbing."

"Sounds cool. You do it every year?"

"I went last year. Can't wait." He pointed elsewhere on the grounds. "Oh, that's the guesthouse. Really nothing to see there."

Dylan scanned the windows. A shadow moved past an upper one, too quick and deliberate to be a cleaning person.

"Can we go to the beach now?"

"Let's have a quick look at the guesthouse, shall we?"

Sean's face fell, but he was a good sport. "Okay."

Dylan stood. Did he glimpse a curtain closing in one of the rooms? Was he seeing things again?

"So nobody is in the guesthouse, right?" He tried to keep his voice casual.

"Nope. Nobody."

But despite Sean's surety, Dylan had seen something. Someone was watching him, and they were using the guesthouse as their vantage point.

They walked along the path by the pond. At the guesthouse, Sean punched a code on the keypad and opened the door. "Here it is."

"This is a guesthouse?"

Sean's brows came together, like he was considering whether he should answer the question. "It *is* the guesthouse."

"Of course. Never mind."

The first floor was probably two or three times the size of the apartment Dylan shared with his mom. And the dustcovers strewn over furniture did nothing to hide the luxurious appointments. Still, it had all the appearance of being empty. So why did he feel someone was nearby?

"Can we go now?" Sean tugged on his arm.

"Sure."

"When can we go to the beach?"

Dylan's chest tightened. How many times had he wished for someone to take him places when his mom was working double shifts? "Tell you what. We can go later today."

Sean's face lit up like Christmas morning. "Really? You promise?"

"I promise." The words slipped out before Dylan could stop them. He was supposed to leave this place, not make commitments to lonely kids.

After retrieving his laptop from his room, Dylan strode out to the gazebo. He settled on the bench he had sat on earlier and opened his laptop. His mother appeared on-screen, and his breath caught in his throat. She looked so alive, so present, that for an instant he forgot she was gone. Then reality crashed back, and he slammed the laptop shut.

His fingers tap-danced on the metal surface. This was it—the moment he'd been both dreading and desperate for since looping that key around his neck.

After steadying his breathing, he reopened the laptop.

"Dylan, if you're watching this, then I'm already dead."

The words hit like a physical blow. She'd known. She'd planned this. While he was going about his normal life, she'd been preparing to speak to him from beyond the grave.

"I love you so much. I'm so sorry for having lied to you all these years. It's for your protection."

He paused the video, his vision blurring. Protection from what? From whom? The threatening note in his pocket felt heavier.

Seeing his mother talking to him, choking up at times, even via video, was too much.

She had to have recorded this during her brief remission period. She appeared thinner than he remembered, her cheekbones more pronounced, but strength still girded her voice, fire still flashed in her eyes. Not the frail woman she'd become in those final weeks, but not the healthy mother from his childhood either.

Did he have it in him to continue? But didn't he owe it to himself—to *her*—to hear what she had to say?

He pressed the arrow to play.

"I know you have a lot of questions. I may not have all the

answers, but I'll tell you what I know. But before I say anything else, please be careful. There aren't a lot of people you can trust at Mirror Estate, but you can trust Phil, er, I should say Fr. Phil."

His pent-up breath whooshed free. At least he had one ally in this place.

She smiled. Her eyes stared at some faraway place, maybe remembering some good times. He pressed pause and wanted to capture that image forever. Then he started the video again.

"Fun fact. He was a Navy SEAL before answering the call to the priesthood."

Dylan's eyebrows shot up. That explained the priest's bearing, his watchful eyes, his way of seeming to assess Dylan like a potential threat. A Navy SEAL turned priest. No wonder his mother trusted him.

"Your most burning question is probably why. Why did I run away? Why did I leave all that? The answer? Well, one day, someone put a note in your dad's shirt pocket. It said to run and hide. It said there was a contract on his head. He wanted to go by himself, but I wouldn't let him."

A chill iced Dylan's blood. A contract? Like in the movies—someone had put a *hit* on his father? But why? His father was a teenager then with hopes of going to college to be a software engineer or a computer programmer.

"Your dad and I uncovered some damaging information. That made some people very unhappy. If he was in danger, I was sure I'd be next. We never found out who warned us."

Pride mixed with his fear. His parents had been brave enough to uncover something important, something dangerous. They'd stood up to people so powerful they could order murders.

"You have the key to a box with some documents inside. We've buried the box somewhere safe. I've attached the drawing of a map to this email so you can find it. It's your leverage for now. But first, let me tell you a secret."

The video froze, buffering.

His lungs burned. Had he been holding his breath? Whatever his mother was about to reveal was big enough to get people killed.

28 YEARS AGO

Maggie counted twelve nervous glances Mickey had thrown toward the dark corner since they'd arrived. Every few seconds, his gaze darted away from her face to scan the shadows between the towering shelves, then back to her, then away again like he expected someone to jump out from behind the encyclopedias.

The library smelled like mold and forgotten stories, and the dusty air scratched the back of her throat each time she breathed. But it was the only place no one ever checked after lights-out, wedged in the back corner behind sagging bookshelves and a half-broken, clangy radiator.

"Mickey." She leaned back against the cold concrete wall, the chill seeping through her thin T-shirt. "What's wrong with you tonight?"

He stood close enough that she could feel the warmth coming off him, but his shoulders were rigid, his hands shoved deep in his pockets. "Nothing's wrong."

"Right. That's why you've looked over your shoulder twelve times since we got here."

"I haven't been counting."

"I have." The flickering emergency light overhead cast his face in alternating shadow and pale-yellow glow. "You're being weird. Weirder than usual."

His jaw tightened. "Can I ask you something? About your family?"

The question hit her sideways. Two years of writing letters in code names and two years of whispered phone calls from hallway pay phones, and he'd never once asked about her family. Everyone at her boarding school thought she was full of it, claiming to have a boyfriend no one ever met. They called him *Mr. Imaginary*. But he was real. And he was here. So why did talking about her family suddenly matter?

"What about them?"

"Your dad, mostly." Mickey's gaze found hers, then slid away again. "What does he actually do?"

"He runs hotels. You know that."

"No, I mean what does he do for them? Like, day-to-day. He travels quite a bit, right?"

Her chest tightened. "Yeah, so? That's his job."

"But there's no website. No press coverage. No interviews with hospitality magazines." Mickey pulled his hands from his pockets, fidgeting with his jacket zipper. "That's not how hotel chains work, Maggie. You ever see his name on anything? A business card? A tax form?"

The radiator clanged again, louder this time, and she jumped. "You're being weird. He's private. That's all. Old school. I mean, yeah, there's stuff I don't know, but he's in the hotel business. That's what he's always said."

"What stuff don't you know?"

"I don't know. That's the point." She pushed off from the wall, stepping toward him. "Why are you asking me this? You sound like you're investigating me."

He rubbed the back of his neck; that telltale gesture that

meant he was holding something back. "I just need to under-stand some things."

"What things?"

"Can you just answer about your dad first?"

She raised her voice without meaning to. "I *did* answer."

When he shushed her, she lowered it again. "He runs hotels. He travels. He's private. What else do you want to know?"

Instead of responding, he walked deeper into their hidden corner, past the bound journals and toward a section where the emergency light barely reached. Wood scraped against wood, then came the soft thud of something being lifted.

"Mickey, what are you—"

He appeared again, carrying a cardboard file box coated in dust that caught the light like gray snow. The way he held it, carefully, like it might explode, made her stomach clench.

"Remember my dad's storage unit?"

"Of course. I drove you there." When Mickey finally found the courage to check out what his father had left in the storage unit, she was the one who drove him, since he had no other way to get across town. She'd sat in the car while he disappeared into the maze of metal doors, emerging half an hour later with three boxes and red-rimmed eyes.

"This was buried in one of the boxes I brought back." He set the box on the low table between two chairs but didn't open it. Instead, he looked at her with an expression she couldn't read. "My dad kept copies of everything. Old case files, photos. Stuff he never turned in."

Her throat felt dry. "Your dad was a good cop. A hero. Why would he keep secrets?"

"Because maybe he didn't trust everyone around him."

Mickey lifted the lid with the same care he might use to defuse a bomb. The smell that wafted up was different from the library's mustiness, sharper, like old ink and cigarette smoke that had been trapped for years.

He laid out the contents piece by piece. Spreadsheets with columns of numbers that meant nothing to her. Blurry photocopies of handwritten journals in cramped script. Several pages of typed reports with "CONFIDENTIAL" stamped across the top in red ink that had faded to rust.

And then the photographs.

Black-and-white, some color, faded to sepia. Men in expensive suits shaking hands outside restaurants she didn't recognize. Groups gathered around tables in what looked like private dining rooms. Surveillance shots taken from a distance, faces circled in red pen.

Her breath caught.

"That's Uncle Charles." She pointed to a photo of a tall, distinguished man with salt-and-pepper hair, caught mid-laugh as he clapped someone on the shoulder. "And this guy..." Her finger moved to another image. "He's my father's cousin. Antonio. We saw him in Italy once, but I wasn't allowed to talk to him. My dad said he was a complicated man."

Mickey's voice was quiet. "His full name's Antonio Marino."

"Yeah. So?"

"He's not just complicated, Maggie. He's connected. Major organized crime. And 'Uncle Charles'?" He pulled out another photograph, this one clearly from a surveillance setup. Charles sat across from two men whose faces had been circled multiple times. "He's been under investigation too."

The words hit her like cold water. "No. There has to be an explanation. My father's not... he's not part of anything like that."

But even as she said it, pieces shifted in her mind. That trip to Italy five years ago, she'd been so excited to meet her dad's extended family, imagining cousins her age and big family dinners like in the movies. Instead, her father had grown increasingly tense as their arrival date approached.

"Stay at the hotel tonight, sweetheart. I have some family business to discuss."

"Can't I come? I want to meet everyone."

"Not tonight. Another time."

But there hadn't been another time. She'd spent the evening staring out their hotel window, glimpsing her father through the restaurant window across the street. He'd sat rigid in his chair while Antonio gestured, flanked by men who could've stepped out of a mob-themed movie. When her father returned to the hotel three hours later, his face had been gray.

She'd thought it was jet lag.

"Maggie?" Mickey's voice seemed to come from far away.

She blinked, refocusing on the documents. "This doesn't mean my dad's involved in anything illegal. Maybe he's just trying to stay away from that world."

He held up a page covered in jagged handwriting and arrows connecting names like a conspiracy theorist's fever dream. "Then explain this."

She took the paper with trembling fingers. The names were a mix of typed labels and handwritten additions. Some she recognized, politicians she'd seen on the news, business leaders her father had mentioned in passing. Others were completely foreign. Three had the word *cop* written next to them in different colored ink. One was labeled *Senator*. Some faces had thick *X*s drawn over them. Others had question marks.

Her father's name was there, written in blue ink with a black question mark beside it.

"This doesn't make sense." Her voice came out as a croak. "Why is his name on here at all?"

"Look at this." He pointed to another document, an organizational chart with government agencies on one side and shell companies on the other. Lines connected them in a web of relationships she couldn't follow. Nicknames were scattered throughout: Scarface, Orchid, Red. "It's not just criminals,

Maggie. It's people in power. People who should be stopping this stuff."

"No." She shook her head so hard her vision blurred. "My dad's not involved in anything illegal. He can't be."

But her hands were shaking now, and the memory of Italy wouldn't leave her alone. Her father's gray face when he returned to the hotel. The way he'd been quiet for the rest of the trip, jumping every time his phone rang. How he'd made her promise never to mention Antonio to anyone back home.

"Family business is complicated, sweetheart. Some things are better left private."

Mickey reached into the box again and removed a manila envelope seemingly newer than the rest. "There's more."

"I don't want to see more."

"You need to."

Two hospital documents slid onto the table. The crisp white paper must've been recently photocopied. Pink hospital birth records, the kind they give new parents. Her vision seemed to split.

One listed a birth time of 2:28 a.m. for Baby A. The other showed 2:38 a.m. for Baby B. Both were girls. Both had the same mother's name listed.

The radiator clanged again, but this time, the sound seemed to come from inside her chest. "What in the world is this?"

"I don't know. But it would appear your mom gave birth to twin girls."

Her fingers numb, she picked up the documents, turning them over and over. Her head knew that, in photocopy form, there was no way to tell if the hospital birth records were forgeries, but her heart kept searching anyway, for some typo, some impossible detail to explain everything away. The hospital letterhead looked real enough. Even the coffee stain on one corner had been faithfully reproduced.

"This can't be real."

Quiet, Mickey watched her with an expression that might have been pity.

"There has to be another explanation." Her voice sounded desperate even to her ears. "Maybe it was a mix-up at the hospital. Paperwork errors happen all the time."

"Maggie." His voice was so gentle it made her chest ache. "What if it's not a mistake?"

She met his eyes for the first time since he'd opened the box. "What do you mean?"

"What if you weren't the only baby?"

The words hung in the air between them like smoke. Her pulse pounded in her ears, drowning out the radiator's clanging, the distant sounds of the orphanage settling around them. She felt like she was falling down an elevator shaft with no bottom in sight.

"What if—" She had to stop and swallow hard before she could continue. "If... if these are real, then what happened to the other baby? And why wouldn't Mommy and Daddy have said anything about her?"

Mickey's face crumpled. "I don't know. But I had to show you. I couldn't keep pretending I didn't know."

She stared at the birth records until the letters blurred together. Baby A. Baby B. Two different times. Two different babies. Both born to her mother.

CHAPTER 18
UNFINISHED QUESTIONS

It was all an act. Everything was an act. Now, Dylan understood.

The realization had hit him like a physical blow as he'd stood in the backyard, staring at his laptop. His mother's face in that video, hollow-eyed and desperate, telling him the truth she'd carried for years.

The photos attached to her email—images of a woman who looked exactly like his mother, but clearly wasn't her. Different clothes, different settings, different moments in time that his mother would have remembered differently. And beneath those photos, the scanned birth records that explained everything.

Baby A. Baby B. Two babies, born minutes apart. One raised by Ralph and Carol. The other supposedly dead.

Except the photos proved she wasn't dead. She was very much alive.

His finger jammed the door chime button repeatedly. He hadn't known he couldn't get back into the house from the backyard without a code. It made sense for security purposes, but right now, it felt like the universe was conspiring to keep him from the confrontation that had been building his entire life.

At last, the door swung open. "Where's the fire?" Uncharacteristic disapproval crept into Max's usually measured tone.

Dylan pushed past the majordomo. "Where is she?"

"Who? Ms. Carol?"

"Yes." Without waiting for a reply, he started yelling. "Carol! Carol!"

"No need to shout." Max's voice carried a sharp edge. "She's in the library."

Dylan stalked toward that room, his pulse hammering in his ears. Max's measured footsteps followed, but Dylan didn't care. All these years of hiding the truth. All those years of playing the grieving mother when she knew. She had to have known.

"I thought you were sincere." His voice cut through the afternoon quiet the moment he entered the library. There she was, reading, her startled eyes now wide. "Thought you really missed my mom. How wrong I was!"

Carol stood up, her face creasing. "What are you talking about? Because I do miss her. Every single day."

"Dylan, you have no right to talk to Ms. Carol like this." Max stepped in the doorway.

"I can talk to her any way I want to." The words came out harsh, but Dylan was past caring about politeness.

The butler opened his mouth to protest, but Carol raised her hand. "Wait outside, please, Max. I'm sure it's just a misunderstanding."

Dylan waited until Max retreated before moving closer to Carol. Close enough to see her genuine confusion or what looked like genuine confusion. "Stop pretending! You said you didn't know why she ran away."

"That's because I didn't know. Still don't." Carol's voice remained steady, but her hands had started to tremble. "I suspect she ran because Ralph didn't approve of Mickey. They never saw eye to eye. Mickey was the son of a policeman, and Ralph came from different stock."

"Really?" Dylan pulled out his phone, his fingers working to open his email. "You or your husband, or maybe both of you drove her away because my mother didn't want anything to do with the criminal enterprise. Your other daughter, though, my mom's twin sister, probably has no qualms about inheriting the family business. Am I right?"

Carol's face went through a series of expressions. The confusion could have been feigned, even the disbelief, before her hand flew to her throat as her eyes went wild with what could only be terror. "Her twin?"

"Yes, I found out." He swiped to the photos first, holding the screen toward Carol. "Someone sent her these. Pictures of a woman who looks exactly like her, but isn't her."

He scrolled through images of a teenage girl, a young woman, recent photos of someone who could have been Mom's double. "She remembered these weren't her photos, weren't her memories. And take a look at the hospital birth records."

Dylan swiped to the documents. "Two babies, born ten minutes apart. Baby A and Baby B. Both girls. Both born to you."

Carol stared at the phone screen as if it were showing her a ghost. Her hand clutched tighter at her throat. "Those are... how did she get...?"

"My mother told me." Dylan's throat closed in on the words. "She was dying. And someone sent her photos of a woman identical to her. Then she remembered the birth records she'd seen years ago and put it all together."

Carol's gaze never left the phone screen, but the blood drained from her face, leaving her skin ashen.

"The baby died," she whispered. One hand still clutched to her throat. The shaky other stretched toward the phone as if to touch the woman. Those fingers fell limp to her lap. "She only lived a few hours. We never even brought her home from the hospital."

"According to who? Because these records show two healthy babies, born ten minutes apart."

Carol pushed off her chair arms, trying to stand, but her legs gave out. Her eyes rolled back, and she slid from the seat like a rag doll.

Dylan dropped his phone and lunged forward, catching her before she hit the floor. All his anger evaporated in a rush of panic. What if she'd had a heart attack? What if he'd caused that?

He lowered her to the carpet, his hands shaking as he felt for her pulse. It was there, rapid but steady.

"Oh dear." Max spoke from the doorway. "I'll get her pills."

Dylan picked up his phone, this time to dial 911. Max's running footsteps echoed down the hallway.

"Nine-one-one, what's your emergency?"

"Why don't you talk to them?" Dylan held the phone out to Max, who had reappeared with a pill bottle.

Max took the phone while gesturing for Dylan to give Carol one of the pills. Then Max relayed the address and asked for Dr. Green to be notified.

Dylan's hands shook as he placed the pill under Carol's tongue.

"They're on the way." Max ended the call. "About three minutes. I'll have Duke send them in when they arrive."

"Does she faint often?" How concerned he sounded!

"Once or twice. It's happened when she's agitated." Max's voice was neutral, but he glanced at the phone still displaying the birth records. "Dylan, I couldn't help but overhear what you said. I don't know where or how you came by that information. But I can bet my life Ms. Carol didn't come up with any evil scheme."

Max knelt beside Carol, checking her pulse with the ease of

someone who'd done this before. "The way I understand it, the twin lived only a few hours. They didn't even bring her home from the hospital. Mr. Ralph didn't want to upset Ms. Carol any more than she already was. I tell you, she was a wreck. If she hadn't had to nurse your mother, she'd have been in bed for weeks."

Dylan's eyebrows knitted together. "But someone sent my mother pictures of her twin. Recent photos showing a woman identical to her."

Max's face went pale. "That's... that's impossible."

Carol's eyelids fluttered open. "My baby?" She barely managed a whisper. "Is she..."

Dylan leaned closer. "What?"

Before she could finish her sentence, the paramedics rushed in, professional and efficient. "Excuse us. Please step back so we have room to work on her."

Dylan stood up, reeling. Her unfinished question hung in the air like smoke. She'd been asking about the twin, the baby she'd thought was dead for over forty years.

But if she genuinely didn't know, if her shock and collapse were real, then who had stolen the baby? And why had Dylan's dying mother been sent proof her twin was still alive?

22 YEARS AGO

"How did they find us?" Maggie whispered, her hands trembling as she pulled clothes from Dylan's dresser and prepared the toddler bag.

"I don't know." Mickey's voice was tight, controlled, but fear heightened its pitch. "Grab the go-bag and get Dylan ready."

The go-bag. They hadn't touched it in over a year. Dust had settled on the canvas handles where it lay in their bedroom closet, a relic from the days when they'd lived like ghosts, always ready to vanish.

Dylan sat on his bedroom floor, building block towers, oblivious to the tension crackling through the house. At two years old, he lived in a world where Mama and Dada could fix anything, where the biggest tragedy was a broken cookie.

"Dylan, sweetie." Maggie picked up the toddler and began changing his pull-up. "We're going on a trip. Can you help Mama pack your favorite toys?"

His face lit up. "Go beach?"

"Sort of." She swallowed the ache in her throat. "Which stuffed animal do you want to bring?"

"Bear!" Dylan hugged his worn teddy bear, the one Mickey

bought him at the hospital gift shop the day he was born. "And truck!"

"Just Bear, honey. We're traveling light." She stuffed a change of clothes into his little backpack, the one with cartoon dinosaurs that he insisted on wearing everywhere.

Mickey appeared in the doorway, his bag slung over his shoulder. He looked so normal, so everyday. But his gaze kept darting to the windows, and his hand rested near his waistband where he kept his gun. "Ready?"

She scooped Dylan into her arms. He was getting so big, so heavy. When had that happened?

"Dada come?" Dylan reached over her shoulder toward Mickey.

"Of course, buddy." Mickey touched his son's cheek, and his expression softened. "Dada's coming too."

The drive felt surreal. Dylan chattered in his car seat, pointing out dogs and trucks and asking, "We there?" every few minutes.

Mickey handed her a slip of paper without taking his focus off the road. "Keep the number, just in case. Chris is Phil's buddy from his SEAL days. We're meeting him at the motel. He's going to help us."

Phil. It'd been too long since she had seen Fr. Phil. She'd asked Mickey once what his relationship with the priest was— why he trusted him so much. He never gave a straight answer. She'd stopped asking. If her husband trusted Phil, then she would too.

"I don't see anyone." The motel parking lot stretched before them, cracked asphalt and flickering neon. Half the letters in the vacancy sign had burned out. "Are you sure this is it? It looks so... so run-down. The neighborhood is sketchy too."

"That's the idea." His knuckles were white on the steering wheel. "I doubt the guy at the front wants to know what goes on in the rooms. I got us a room earlier. The key is in the console there. We'll wait in the room."

He parked in the back, away from the few cars scattered around the lot. The silence felt heavy after the engine shut off.

"We there?" Dylan sounded disappointed.

"Not yet, sweetie." Maggie unbuckled him, her fingers fumbling with the car seat straps. "We're just stopping to rest."

The motel room smelled like stale cigarettes and industrial carpet cleaner. Dylan wrinkled his nose but didn't complain. Mickey set the chain lock and checked the window while she tried to make the best of it.

"Look, Dylan. You can see the parking lot from here. Maybe we'll see some big trucks drive by."

But Mickey drew the drapes. "Sorry, we don't want to be a target."

"Well, Dylan, why don't you play with Bear, then?"

Mickey kept checking his phone, checking his watch, checking the parking lot through the drapes.

The waiting stretched. Dylan grew restless, wanting to explore, wanting snacks, wanting to know when they were leaving. Maggie played patty-cake with him, sang his favorite songs, anything to keep him occupied and calm.

"Mama, hungy."

"I know, baby. We'll get food soon."

"Fishy!" He bounced.

She rummaged in the toddler bag, dug out a bag of Goldfish crackers, and gave him a few.

Mickey's phone buzzed. He glanced at it and stood. "I'm going to check outside. Chris should be here any minute."

"Mickey—"

"Lock the door behind me. Don't open it for anyone but me or Chris."

The door clicked shut. She turned the dead bolt and settled Dylan on the bed with his bear. A television in the next room yammered through the thin walls. Then canned laughter from some sitcom rang out.

"Where Dada?" Dylan started to sound cranky.

"Just outside, honey. He'll be right back."

But minutes passed. Dylan fussed, tired and hungry and confused by this strange place. She tried to distract him, but her anxiety was growing. Where was Mickey? Where was Chris?

Then came the sounds. Not quite like firecrackers, but sharp and sudden. Dylan's head popped up.

"Just firecrackers, sweetie." Her heart raced. She pulled Dylan closer to her on the bed, away from the window. "Let's play a quiet game."

More sounds. Definitely not firecrackers. Tires squealing. Shouting.

Dylan started to whimper. "Dada!"

"Dada will be back soon." The lie felt like glass in her throat. She had to look. Had to see.

She crossed to the window and peered through the curtains. Her world tilted.

Mickey was lying just outside the door, clutching his belly, blood, so much blood, pooling beneath him.

"Oh no. Oh no." She grabbed the phone and ran outside, Dylan's cries following her.

"Mickey!"

He looked up at her, his face gray in the parking lot lights. "Maggie…"

"I'm calling 911—"

He shook his head. "Close… the… door."

"But—"

"Close… the… door." His voice was urgent despite its weakness. "Dylan."

Another round of popping sounds erupted from somewhere in the parking lot. She ran back inside, slammed the door, and threw the dead bolt. Dylan was standing on the bed, sobbing.

"Mama! Mama, where Dada?"

She scooped him up, covering him with her body as she dove for the floor beside the bed. "It's okay, baby. It's okay."

But it wasn't okay. Nothing was okay.

Lord, help us!

The popping sounds continued, then stopped. Silence stretched, heavy and terrifying. Dylan's sobs turned to hiccups against her shoulder.

Then all was quiet except for a curse from a stranger.

"We're too late."

Another voice, lower: "That your wife and son?"

She couldn't hear, but Mickey must have nodded or said yes.

Then footsteps, voices she didn't recognize speaking in low, urgent tones. Her heartbeat slowed enough that she could think. These had to be Phil's friends. They had to be.

She stood, Dylan still in her arms.

"Dada?" Dylan pointed toward the door.

"He's... Dada's outside, honey." She put her son on the bed before she headed to open the door. "Stay here."

A bulky man was squatting beside Mickey, pressing what looked like a sheet—when had someone gotten a sheet?—against Mickey's abdomen. Another man stood guard, scanning the parking lot.

"Are you Chris?" she asked.

"Chris Stallings, ma'am. That's Kurt, another buddy." He didn't look at her, focused on Mickey. "I'm sorry. Got held up in traffic. Took care of those goons out there."

Traffic. Such a normal everyday word for whatever had happened in this parking lot.

"Mickey, you'll be fine." She said it for Dylan as much as for Mickey, but the look on Chris's face told her everything she didn't want to know.

"Chris..." Mickey's voice was fading. "Protect them, please."

"You have my word."

Mickey tilted his head toward her and Dylan, such effort in that simple movement. "Take care... of Dylan." Each word seemed to cost him. "Tell him... I love him."

"You can tell him yourself." She was crying now, couldn't help it. "You'll be fine."

Mickey smiled, so weak, so loving. "I love you. Be strong."

"I love you. Don't leave us."

She held his hand, felt it grow cold. She didn't know how long she sat there, whispering prayers and promises and love into the stale motel air.

When Chris touched her shoulder, she already knew.

"Maggie, I'm sorry, but he's gone."

"No." The word came out flat, empty. Dylan's cries floated from the room, but she couldn't move. Couldn't think.

"We need to go."

Out of the corner of her eye, she caught Dylan in the arms of a man. She snapped back to awareness. "Hey, that's my son! Where are you taking him?"

But Kurt was already walking toward the car, Dylan looking back at her with wide eyes.

"Mama, come!"

She followed, her legs unsteady. When had Kurt put a car seat in his truck? When had he prepared for this?

"Dada come?" Dylan blinked up at her as Kurt buckled him in.

Maggie swallowed hard. "Dada... Dada has to stay here."

The boy's brow furrowed. "No. Dada come too."

His little hands stretched toward the door, his voice wobbling. "No! Come, Dada!"

Her chest ached. She reached in to smooth his curls, steadied her voice. "Dada can't right now, baby. He's sleeping."

How do you explain death to a two-year-old? How do you make sense of the senseless?

"Hey, lady, we need to go." Chris's voice was gentle but

urgent. "Those guys aren't working alone. You want to be here when their friends show up?"

She looked back at the motel room door, still open, showing a slice of the life that just ended. Mickey was there, and she was leaving him. Leaving him with strangers in a place that smelled like cigarettes and despair.

"I can't leave him."

"There's nothing you can do for him now." Chris touched her shoulder. "He wanted you to take care of your son. Can't do that if something happens to you too."

Dylan was watching her through the truck window, thumb in his mouth, Bear clutched in his other arm. Waiting for Mama to make everything okay the way she always did.

She ran back to Mickey one last time, kissed his forehead, whispered, "I love you" into hair that still smelled like his shampoo. Then she ran to the truck before she could change her mind.

As they pulled away, Chris spoke into his phone. "Yeah, it's done. What do you want me to do about...?" She didn't care about the rest. Nothing mattered anymore.

Dylan had fallen asleep, exhausted by tears and confusion. His little chest rose and fell, so peaceful, so trusting that tomorrow would make sense even when today didn't.

The truck started moving, carrying them away from everything they'd known, everything they'd been. In the side mirror, she glimpsed Kurt's silhouette in the motel doorway before the darkness swallowed it whole.

"Where are we going?" she asked Chris.

"Somewhere safe. That's all you need to know right now."

Dylan stirred in his sleep, muttering, "Dada!"

She reached back to touch his hand. "Dada loves you, baby. Dada loves you so much."

But Mickey was gone, and somehow, she had to figure out how to be enough for both of them.

CHAPTER 19

AFTER THE COLLAPSE

The same smell. Every hospital had the same antiseptic smell masking something Dylan didn't want to think about. He'd spent too many hours in places like this, watching his mother's treatments fail one by one. Now Carol was behind one of these doors, and he couldn't shake the question that gnawed at him since the ambulance arrived: Had his accusations put her here?

Fr. Phil had arrived not long after Max's summons. Townsend showed up next, reminding Dylan that he wasn't officially the next of kin. Fr. Phil was the agent named as her healthcare proxy.

A doctor came in and beelined for the priest. It appeared the family and the priest were familiar figures here. After a brief, private consultation, the doctor left.

"She's fine. Nothing serious," Fr. Phil announced. "They want to keep her overnight for observation. Depending on her symptoms, they may run more tests. But it's looking good."

Dylan's shoulders sagged with relief he hadn't expected to feel. The last few hours had been a blur, but seeing Carol collapse stripped away everything except the fear that he'd killed the woman who might be his only real family left. The same fear he'd carried through every one of his mother's hospital stays—that this time, she wouldn't come home.

He'd been starting to like Carol. The way she'd looked at him when he arrived at the estate, like he was some kind of answer to her prayers. The stories she'd told about his mother, painted a picture that matched the kind, gentle woman who'd raised him. Even her obvious guilt over the past felt genuine.

But then, those photos. That video. The twin sister who might still be alive.

Was Carol's remorse all an act? She hadn't had to send Townsend to find him. If she'd wanted to keep the family secrets buried, letting him live his anonymous life would have been easier. But what if she'd brought him here for some other reason? What if—

"Thank God!" Max crossed himself, cutting through Dylan's spiraling thoughts.

A nurse told them Carol was asleep. "You all should get some rest and come back later."

"I'm going to anoint her, and then I need to go. Unless something changes, I'll plan to visit the estate soon." The priest headed to the elevator.

"I'll see her back at the estate too." With that, Townsend left. The man had barely stayed long enough to hear that Carol was stable. For someone who'd been with the family forever, his concern seemed oddly... professional.

Max insisted on staying.

"Let's grab a bite," Dylan suggested, and the butler agreed after a brief hesitation.

The episode back at the house seemed to have loosened Max up. No jacket, no tie. Even his posture had changed from ramrod straight to a relaxed slouch. They followed the signs to the cafeteria. Unlike the hospital Dylan's mother had been in, this small one didn't have a food court for visitors and a café for employees.

As they walked, an air-care helicopter approached the roof, so they must medevac anyone with serious injuries or illnesses to more sophisticated hospitals.

Max only got a cup of coffee, but Dylan bought a sandwich to go with his coffee.

"How can you eat that?" The man eyed the package.

Dylan finished unwrapping his ham sandwich. "What? It's a sandwich."

"It's probably been sitting there for days."

"Look, not everyone has a daughter who can cook like Lorraine. Not everyone eats fresh food every day. I've eaten leftovers a lot." He finished unwrapping it and took a big bite. "Let's say the twin did die at the hospital. Why would my mother make this up?"

"I never said she made anything up. I don't even know the whole story. I just overheard you yelling at Ms. Carol."

"Fair enough." Instead of recounting what he'd heard, Dylan showed Max the image attachments on his phone. "See, here she's shopping, here she's reading, and here she's at some party."

Max studied the images, his weathered face creased. "I've heard you can Photoshop anything these days. These might not be real."

"True, but there's a video too." Dylan tapped his screen. "Here. This looks like a proof-of-life video. She's holding a copy of the *New York Times* to show the date. Too bad there's no audio."

Max's eyes widened. "While I haven't seen your mom in years, this woman looks just like a young Ms. Carol." He frowned. "But, Dylan, think about the logistics of what you're suggesting. If there were a twin, and if she survived, someone would have had to orchestrate an elaborate deception. The doctor, the nurses, the hospital staff—they'd all have to be in on it. And for what? To steal a baby from a crime family?"

A flicker of doubt wormed its way into Dylan's chest, but he forced it down.

Max shook his head. "That's not how these things work. You don't cross the Marinos and live to tell about it."

Dylan bit into his sandwich and took his time to chew. "Maybe it wasn't crossing them. Maybe it was someone they trusted."

"And where has this supposed twin been all these years? If she's working with the family's enemies, why wait until now to surface? Why not use her against Ms. Carol decades ago?" Max leaned forward. "You're looking for complicated explanations when the simple one is right there. Your mother ran away, just like Ms. Carol said. These photos could be anyone."

"But the resemblance—"

"Could be a distant cousin, someone hired to look like her, or a coincidence." Max's voice grew gentler. "I understand you're trying to make sense of everything. But sometimes the truth is simpler than we want it to be."

Dylan frowned. Max's arguments made sense, but something still felt off. "Here's my theory. Let's assume the twin is alive. My mom wanted nothing to do with the criminal enterprise, but her sister didn't mind. So, they got rid of the righteous daughter. That's what I was thinking." A thought flitted through his mind, but he couldn't quite grasp the significance of it.

"Are you sure you're not just trying to shirk your responsibilities?"

"What responsibilities?"

"Why do you think Ms. Carol wanted to find your mother? Your mom is gone. But she found you, the rightful heir. This is your new reality. She's getting on in years. She's done a lot to right the wrongs of the Marino family. Don't you want to carry on building that legacy?"

What could he say to that? This wasn't anything he had considered.

Max twisted his coffee mug between his palms. "Let's say the other girl survived, didn't die. Who raised her? Where is she? She was never at Mirror Estate. Not even after your mother ran away. Think about it: If what you thought was true, when your mother took off, wouldn't Ms. Carol and Mr. Ralph have brought the other girl home to take her place?"

Dylan dropped his head to his hands, pulled at his hair. Too much had happened too quickly. "You're right. It's fishy. Let's just assume she is alive, though. Someone close to the family, someone who had access to the babies, would've had to smuggle her out of the hospital. And somehow convinced Carol and her husband that the baby died."

"To what end? Baby abduction?"

From what he knew of the Marinos from the beginning… "Max, you've been with the family so long. Do you believe they got out of that life? Fr. Phil hinted some ties were dangerous to cut. What do you think?"

"I don't know how they did it. It's probably easier to deal with the law. I assume you turn yourself in and that's that. But the ones on the other side of the law aren't that easy to deal with. So, you've got me. I do know the business is legitimate now."

"What can you tell me about Townsend?"

He shrugged. "He's been with the family forever. They go way back. Mr. Ralph used to call him his number one."

But what about Townsend's quick departure earlier? "You said Townsend and Ralph went way back?"

"That's right. Like I said, his number one." Max paused, coffee cup halfway to his lips. "Why?"

"Just curious about the family dynamics." But in every crime movie Dylan had ever seen, the boss's "number one" wasn't just an employee. He was the enforcer, the problem solver, the one who handled the family's dirty work.

What if Townsend hadn't been sent to find Dylan to welcome him home? What if he'd been sent for a different reason?

The thought that had been nagging at him crystallized, and he understood why something had felt wrong about Townsend from the moment they'd met. He shot up onto his feet. "I need to check something."

14 YEARS AGO

Marge Beaumont had been playing the dutiful daughter for years. Years of "yes, ma'am" and "of course, ma'am" while the slow poison did its work. Now, watching the woman who'd stolen her from her real family waste away in this private bed, she could barely contain her satisfaction.

"They call you the ghost, Marge." The old woman wheezed.

Marge chuckled, adjusting the morphine drip with practiced ease. "Not very imaginative."

"My days are numbered. You'll take over now."

"No, no, I'm not ready. You'll live!" The lie came as smoothly as breathing. She'd perfected her concerned-daughter act, even as she'd been increasing the arsenic doses in Liz's, her surrogate mother's, evening tea. Each day brought her closer to this moment, closer to claiming what should have been hers from the beginning.

Now, the throne was hers. Practically.

"Remember what I told you about the cop and the traitor? The ledgers, the chart. You must recover those."

The frail body on the bed in no way resembled the formidable crime boss most people feared. But then, Liz hadn't been running things for years. Marge had. Ever since she'd understood what the Marino name meant, what had been stolen from her, she'd been maneuvering herself into position. By twenty, she was handling negotiations. By twenty-five, she was making the real decisions while her "mother" took credit.

"I know your plan. I'll get it taken care of." She had plans to do a whole lot more than that. Plans that didn't include following orders from a dying woman who'd built her empire on kidnapping and lies.

"Have you found your double?"

"Won't be long now. I already got the pictures, the videos. Just waiting for the perfect time." The words came easily, but something twisted in her chest. She'd been watching Maggie for years, first with the intention of eliminating the twin who'd gotten the life that should have been hers.

But watching her twin struggle as a single mother, seeing her gentleness with Dylan, the way she'd removed herself from anything connected to the Marino name... Her twin had chosen poverty and anonymity over power and wealth. It should have made Marge despise her more. Instead, it had made her curious. Made her hesitate when the moment came to act.

She pushed the feeling aside. Sentiment was weakness, and weakness got you killed in this business.

"Good. The treasures..."

Then again came the mumbling about buried loot and family legends. She'd heard it enough. Treasures or not, she'd reclaim Mirror Estate, not for some mythical inheritance, but because it belonged to her bloodline. Because Carol Marino lived there, comfortable and guilt-ridden, while Marge had been raised by the woman who'd torn their family apart.

She'd heard the stories: how Liz had convinced everyone the second twin had died, how she'd taken the "dead" baby to raise as her weapon against the Marinos. How she'd filled Marge's childhood with hatred and plans for revenge.

But now, looking at this withered shell... well, the ultimate revenge wasn't destroying her twin's—and her own—family. It was taking everything back and doing it better than any of them ever had.

"You rest now. I'll go have a chat with our beloved senator." Marge kissed the old woman's forehead, tasting the salt of impending death. "Time to collect on old debts and make new arrangements."

2 WEEKS AGO

Marge stood at the penthouse suite's floor-to-ceiling windows, Mirror Estate's sprawling grounds in the distance. The hotel had been the perfect choice, close enough to observe her target, far enough to remain invisible. Registering under Maria Rossi raised no red flags, and the corner suite offered an unobstructed view of what should've been her childhood home.

The chessboard on the mahogany table behind her held a game in progress, white pieces positioned for victory. She'd been playing both sides for weeks now, working through every possible scenario. Her psychology degree taught her the theory, but decades in the criminal underworld taught her the practice —people were predictable if you knew which buttons to push.

The encrypted phone buzzed against her ear as the connection from China crackled to life.

"Status?" Her breath fogged the glass when she spoke.

"He needs more convincing."

Her free hand swept across the chessboard, scattering the pieces across the polished wood. The clatter echoed through the suite. The satisfying sound did nothing to ease her frustration.

"Use leverage, anything. Make him cooperate. We have lots of friends in that part of China. The triads and others in our pocket. They'll give you a hand, if necessary." She sidestepped the chaos of ivory and ebony pieces now scattered like fallen soldiers.

"What's your plan? You can't be thinking of using his notes. We don't have the capability to make any kind of biological weapon. Besides, the Chinese government wouldn't look kindly on you stealing their research."

She stooped to collect the pieces, setting them back on their squares. Each piece had its place, its purpose, its inevitable fate. "That's not your concern. Just get it done."

She hung up and stared at the reassembled board. Everything was proceeding according to plan, but even the best-laid schemes could unravel. Dylan might not react as she'd predicted. Charles might prove more stubborn than anticipated. Family psychology was always the most complex variable.

But that's what insurance was for.

The pieces were in position. The game was about to begin.

CHAPTER 20
THE BOX

The orphanage grounds stretched before Dylan, silent and abandoned, but he couldn't shake the feeling that unseen eyes were watching his every move. His mother's map led to this place, to secrets buried long ago, and he was beginning to understand that some family legacies were worth killing for.

The late afternoon sun cast long shadows across the weathered brick buildings. Spanish moss draped from the oaks like funeral shrouds, and the air hung thick with humidity and the scent of decay. This place had been abandoned for years, but he could almost sense the echoes of children's voices, could imagine his father as a teenage boy walking these same paths.

His father had lived here. Slept in one of those dormitories. Eaten in that crumbling cafeteria. Dylan studied the ruins, trying to picture his father young and grieving, finding refuge with Fr. Bob after losing everything. *Did you know even then that you'd fall in love with a Marino? Did you have any idea what it would cost you?*

The shovel felt heavier than it should have as he approached the back grounds. Duke, the chauffeur and handyman, had looked at him strangely when he'd asked to borrow it, along with the heavy-duty gloves, but hadn't asked questions. The handyman probably assumed Dylan was helping with a landscaping project.

If only it were so simple.

The willow tree dominated the far corner, its drooping branches creating a natural curtain that would hide his activities from any casual observer. He pulled out his phone again, double-checking the map his mother had drawn. The *X* was positioned about six feet from the tree's massive trunk, next to a small stone marker.

There. A weathered granite stone, no bigger than a shoebox and buried in the overgrown grass. No inscription, nothing to mark its significance to anyone but his parents. He knelt beside it, his breath quickened.

What if someone saw him? What if the box wasn't here? What if Mom was wrong about everything?

The first thrust of the shovel bit into the earth. The ground was firm, but the soil felt slightly softer here, as if it had once been disturbed and had settled over the years. Dylan worked methodically, keeping the noise to a minimum while fighting the urge to look over his shoulder.

Sweat beaded on his forehead despite the late afternoon breeze. Every sound made him freeze, the distant traffic humming, the bird calling, the leaves rustling. He felt exposed, vulnerable, like a target painted on his back. Someone could walk by. Or worse, whoever had been watching him might appear.

Better focus. Just dig.

Six inches down. Twelve. Eighteen. The hole was getting deeper, but exposing nothing but dark soil and the occasional root. His shoulders began to ache, and doubt crept in. Maybe his mother had been confused in those final days. Maybe the cancer had affected her memory more than he'd realized.

Then, a metallic clang. The shovel struck something solid, and the sound seemed to echo across the empty grounds.

Dylan's breath caught. He dropped to his knees, pushed the shovel aside, and used his gloved hands to brush away the remaining dirt. Soon, he exposed a corner of dull gray metal, steel, by the look of it. He cleared more soil, unearthing the outline of a medium-sized lockbox.

He worked it free, the box heavier than he'd expected, the metal thick, substantial, built to withstand weather and time. A sturdy padlock secured the latch. He bet the key around his neck, his mother's final gift, would open this.

His father hid this. His father buried his discoveries here, in the place where he'd found safety as a boy. *How long did you carry these secrets, Dad? How long did you know what you were up against?*

Dylan surveyed the empty grounds, his paranoia spiking. The box seemingly radiated danger, broadcasting its importance to anyone watching. He couldn't open it out here. Too risky. Too exposed.

The chapel. A sign had directed people to the basement restrooms when he visited Fr. Phil earlier. The priest would be busy with evening prayers or pastoral duties. Dylan could slip in, find somewhere private, and then discover what his parents died protecting.

He hefted the box, its weight unnerving. Whatever was inside was substantial. Documents, yes, but something more. Something worth killing for.

The walk back to the chapel felt endless. Every car on the distant road made his pulse spike. Every shadow between the buildings hid potential threats. The box grew heavier with each step, and he switched it from arm to arm to give his muscles a break.

The chapel doors were unlocked, as always. He slipped inside, breathing in the familiar scent of incense and old wood. The sanctuary was empty except for two elderly women praying the rosary in the front pew, their voices a soft murmur in the sacred space.

He approached the basement as quietly as possible, his footsteps echoing on the wooden stairs despite his efforts. The lower level was a maze of storage rooms and meeting spaces, all empty at this hour. Across from the restrooms, just as he'd remembered, stacked cardboard boxes and abandoned furniture filled a small alcove.

Perfect.

Dylan set the lockbox on a pile of boxes, his hands shaking as he pulled the key from beneath his shirt. The chain was warm against his neck, heated by his body and his anxiety.

He hesitated. Once he opened this, everything would change. There'd be no going back to the simple grief of a son who'd lost his mother. This would make him part of something larger, something dangerous.

But his mom wanted him to know.

The key clicked into the lock. He turned it, the mechanism released, and he lifted the lid.

The smell hit him first, old paper, leather, and something else. The metallic tang of fear, maybe, or the mustiness of secrets too long buried. Inside, the box was organized with deliberate precision, a thick manila envelope labeled *Evidence – LR* on top.

LR? The *R* must stand for Roche, so the *L* would be for Leon, his father's middle name, but—ah, this had to be his grandfather's initials. Dylan's middle name was Michael, after his father. His mom might have mentioned it was a family tradition.

So, these were his grandfather's discoveries, the case he'd been building before his death. Beneath the envelope, three leather-bound ledgers, their covers worn smooth by handling. He opened the first one, and a chill iced his blood. Page after page of transactions, amounts, dates, names. And there, in the margins of nearly every page, a name, Charles Townsend, was circled and highlighted.

Notes about "collections." Instructions for "territorial adjustments." References to "problem elimination" and "permanent solutions." This wasn't just evidence of the family's criminal activities. It was proof that their trusted lawyer had been the architect of it all.

Dylan's hands shook as he flipped the pages. Townsend hadn't just been Ralph's attorney. He'd been the enforcer, the strategist, the one who'd made the machine run smoothly. He had been Ralph's number one after all. And somehow, Dylan's father discovered it all.

The second ledger was worse. Bank accounts, shell companies, money-laundering operations that stretched from Florida to Europe. Amounts that made Dylan's head spin, millions of dollars flowing through legitimate businesses, washed clean by a network of lawyers and accountants who knew how to hide dirty money.

Photos came next. Surveillance shots his grandfather must have taken during his investigation. Men in expensive suits shaking hands outside restaurants. Groups gathered around tables in private dining rooms. Some faces Dylan didn't recognize, but others made his stomach drop.

There was Townsend, years younger but unmistakable, sitting across from two men whose faces had been circled in red ink multiple times. Another photo showed him leaving a warehouse, briefcase in hand, face grim.

You weren't just investigating them, Grandpa. You were building a case. You were going to take them all down.

The investigative notes were the most chilling of all. Leon's careful documentation of crimes, connections, and corruption, written in a thick, beat-up journal that must've been carried everywhere. Entry after entry detailed meetings, conversations overheard, suspicious activities observed. Names Dylan recognized from the news—politicians, judges, business leaders. All connected through the decades by a web of money and violence.

Leon was building a case systematically. Every detail documented. Every connection mapped.

And at the center of it all, the Marino family. But not Ralph and Carol. Ralph was listed as "turned" in the notes, marked with question marks and uncertainty about their true loyalties. Curiously, Townsend was listed as "turned" with a question mark.

What did it mean?

The final items were bank account information, complete with numbers and balances and a question mark next to offshore accounts with a crossed-off name. So Leon suspected the criminal empire had hidden money in offshore accounts, but he couldn't access those.

At the bottom, a single photograph made Dylan's breath catch. A couple, probably from the 1970s, standing outside a small church. The woman wore a simple dress and held a bouquet. The man wore a suit, looking worse for wear. With them were two boys, one somewhere around five years old with a gap-toothed grin, the other a teenager with wavy shoulder-length hair that screamed 1970s.

On the back, "A new beginning, Leon and Teresa."

Dylan studied the faces. The little boy had to be Mickey. But who was the teenager? His father had no brother that he knew of, and yet, something about the teen's eyes seemed familiar.

A sound from upstairs made him freeze. Footsteps on the chapel floor. Someone was up there, moving with purpose rather than devotion.

Dylan's pulse spiked. He had to get out of here. Had to take this evidence somewhere safe, somewhere he could figure out what to do with it. The authorities? But how many of them were compromised? His grandfather's notes suggested the corruption went deep, spread wide through law enforcement and government.

He returned everything to the box, his movements precise despite his terror. The key went around his neck, the weight of it heavier now that he understood its significance.

As he closed the lid, footsteps descended the basement stairs.

Please be Fr. Phil. Please be anyone but—

"So, you've unearthed your mother's treasures."

Dylan turned toward the voice, slamming the box shut, his heart stopping as his gaze went straight to the gun in Charles Townsend's hand.

CHAPTER 21
THE TWIN

Dylan's world tilted as his gaze locked onto the gun. The man he'd trusted, who'd flown him here in luxury, who'd spoken so kindly about family, was pointing a weapon at him in a basement that now felt like a tomb.

"What are you doing with that?" The words came out as a croak, his throat dry as sand.

"I knew you'd find those ledgers." Townsend's voice was steady, though something lay underneath. Regret, maybe even pain. "You should have stayed away like your mother did."

The lawyer held the gun with practiced ease, not wavering, not shaking. This wasn't the first time he'd trained a weapon on someone. The realization hit like a physical blow.

"Now, give those to me, and you won't get hurt." Townsend gestured toward the box with his free hand.

Dylan's hands shot up, his mind reeling. "Like I'd believe you."

"Our two families go way back, Dylan." Something almost pleading glossed Townsend's voice. "For the sake of your mother and your grandfather, I guarantee your safety so long as you give me the box. You can't do much without evidence."

Tension coiled in Dylan's chest. The evidence in the box painted Townsend as a criminal mastermind, but the man's eyes suggested a different story. Desperation, not malice. Fear, not cruelty.

"What are you going to do?" How steady his own voice sounded! "Kill me like you killed my parents?"

Townsend winced. "I didn't kill your parents. I warned them."

The words hung in the air. Dylan blinked. Had he misheard? "What?"

"I warned your father. Told him to run. I never expected your mother to go with him."

Before Dylan could respond, before he could process this, movement in his peripheral vision made him turn.

And his world shattered.

A woman emerged from the bathroom across the hall—and he was seeing his mother. The same delicate features, the same way of holding her head, the same gentle slope of her shoulders. But this woman moved differently, like a predator, confident and deadly. And she was holding a gun.

"Mom?" The word slipped out before he could stop it, raw with hope and confusion and desperate longing.

Townsend's expression tensed, his weapon swinging toward the new arrival. "What are you doing here? You're supposed to stay away."

The woman smiled, and the expression transformed her face into something cold and alien. "Why should I? I want to meet my nephew."

Dylan's legs nearly gave out. The resemblance was impossible, perfect, like looking at his mother through a funhouse mirror that reflected everything except her soul. The woman's eyes held no warmth, no kindness, no trace of the gentle spirit that had raised him.

"It was you." His voice came out as a whisper. "You're who's been watching me. I saw you."

She laughed, a sound like breaking glass. "So, you weren't as unaware as I thought you'd be. It was so much fun to see you talking to your mommy." Her voice took on a mocking singsong quality. "Did you really think your mommy was talking to you in your dreams?"

The voice. That voice in his room, the one he'd thought was his mother reaching out from beyond. His stomach lurched. "*You* were in my room?"

"I didn't have to be there. Technology can be amazing." She gestured with her gun, as casual as pointing out interesting architecture. "A few hidden cameras, some voice modulation software, and you were talking to thin air like a crazy person. The look on your face when you thought you were having a spiritual experience…" She savored the words. "Priceless."

Dylan's knees buckled, and he grabbed the cardboard boxes to stay upright. Those tender moments, when he'd thought his mother was somehow reaching out to comfort him from beyond, had been for twisted entertainment?

"Poor little Dylan," she crooned, "so desperate to hear from his dead mama, he'd believe anything. I should have recorded it for posterity."

"Marge, you need to leave." Townsend cut through her mockery. "Your mom…"

"Mom's been dead for fourteen years," Marge snapped, her expression shifting to something darker, more dangerous. "And of course, my real mother probably wanted me to be a weakling like Maggie."

The attorney's face hardened. "Your mom wouldn't have wanted this."

Her laugh was pure venom. "You don't know anything about her. You're just as weak as the others. Why do you think she snatched me? Poor Charlie really bought into her story of wanting a baby so badly." She shook her head in mock pity. "Truth is, you never knew your sister."

Sister. The word hit like a sledgehammer. Townsend's sister had stolen one of the twins.

Townsend said nothing, but his jaw clenched, the muscle in his cheek twitched.

"Cat got your tongue?" Marge pressed, clearly enjoying his discomfort. "Your father passed the mantle to his daughter, not his son! Imagine that?"

So, those were the family dynamics. Townsend wasn't just the family lawyer. He was part of the Marino crime family. His sister had stolen Marge, evidently raised her to be evil, and she somehow ended up running the criminal empire herself.

"You still think you have authority here?" Marge snickered. "Still think your opinion matters? Let me remind you who's been in charge for the last fourteen years." Her smile turned predatory. "They call me the Ghost for a reason, Uncle Charlie. I'm the one giving orders now."

Both guns swung toward each other. Townsend and Marge faced off across the space, weapons trained with deadly intent. The basement air felt thick, charged with violence.

Dylan pressed against the wall to make himself as small as possible. With his phone in his pocket, he couldn't call for help. Even if he could, he'd be shot long before help arrived.

They seemed to have forgotten him. He inched his right foot forward, testing whether he could edge toward the stairs.

"Don't even think about it." Marge swung her gun barrel toward him without taking her gaze off Townsend. "We're just getting to the good part of the family reunion."

Dylan froze, his heartbeat thundering so hard they must all hear it. "What do you want? Did you send those pictures to my mom?"

Marge's smile was pure predator. "You don't understand. See, your grandfather wanted out. A traitor! Can you believe it?

Charlie was ranting to his sister about Ralph's change of heart. Little did he know, his dear sister was already planning to take over."

She gestured toward Townsend with her gun. "And then they hatched this grand plan. Steal a twin, continue the bloodline, hide her... raise her *correctly* to lead the family. At the right moment, she'd assume the other twin's identity and claim what was rightfully hers."

Dylan pivoted to Marge. "So, Baby A was plan A. What was plan B?"

Marge's attention shifted to him, her eyes lighting up. "Can't you guess? I tried to lure her back here to retrieve the stuff they had hidden. I thought she'd want to meet her twin sister, figured family sentiment might override her fear."

Her gaze shifted back and forth from him to Townsend.

"I threatened her with that proof-of-life video, thinking she wouldn't want me dead. Sure, I knew she was sick, but I figured she'd find a way if she cared about saving her twin."

She shrugged. "Imagine my surprise when she chose to protect her precious son instead. And then she up and died on me before I could try a different approach. Guess the cancer was worse than I thought."

The cruelty in her voice knotted Dylan's stomach. She'd tortured his dying mother with the possibility of a sister's murder, all as part of some twisted game. "You monster! You were disappointed that she died before you could torment her more."

The evidence in the box had implicated Townsend as a criminal enforcer, but he'd also warned Dylan's father to run. "I don't understand. Were you hunting my parents or protecting them?"

"I was trying to protect them." Townsend's gun hand wobbled.

Marge snorted. "That's why my mother had to improvise

with plan B, and he's been the one running interference ever since. So many times, Mom wanted me to claim my prize. He wouldn't allow it."

Her voice rose. "You know what the trouble is? You're all weaklings when it comes to family. Mom wouldn't give the order to terminate him when she should have long ago. And you"—she faced Townsend again—"you couldn't take care of one weak child."

"I protected Dylan because he's family," Townsend said. "Families stick together. That used to mean something."

"How touching." Marge's sarcasm grated. "Still playing the family-loyalty card. You think that gives you standing here? That your opinion matters?"

"I'm still your uncle. I'm still part of this family."

"You're a rat." Marge lurched closer. "A federal informant who sold out his own blood for a deal with the government. Mom should have put a bullet in your head years ago instead of listening to your pathetic appeals about family."

So, Townsend was an FBI informant. That explained his desperation to get the evidence. Maybe some crimes in those ledgers weren't covered by his immunity deal.

"Marge, listen." Townsend drew himself into a rigid posture. "We don't want this. Let's just burn the box. Destroy the evidence. And walk away."

Marge's smile was pure venom as she swung her gun back toward him. "I don't think so, Uncle Charlie. I've waited years for this moment." Her finger moved to the trigger. "And you've been protecting the wrong twin."

CHAPTER 22

SHOWDOWN

Dylan's limbs quaked as Marge's finger tightened on the trigger. Townsend had saved his parents' lives by warning them. Dylan couldn't let the man die now, not when Dylan understood the truth.

God, please. I don't know what to do. Help me.

The silent prayer rose from somewhere deep in his chest, desperate and raw. He'd never felt so helpless, so out of his depth. Two guns pointed at each other across a basement that felt smaller by the second, and he was caught in the middle with nothing but words.

Please show me what to say. What to do.

"Tell me how you vanished from the hallway!" The words tumbled out before he could think them through, anything to break Marge's focus, to buy precious seconds. "I saw you disappear."

Her gaze flicked to him. What was that in her eyes? Annoyance at the interruption? Pleasure with his desperation? "Oh, you don't know your way around the house, do you? Hidden doors, secret passageways. Mom made me memorize every one of them when I was a child."

If Dylan survived this, Sean would be thrilled to find those hidden passages. But right now, Dylan needed something else, something bigger, to distract her.

The video. Mom mentioned something else in the video.

"You pull the trigger, you'll never learn where my mom stashed the treasure." His voice gained strength, even as fear twisted in his gut.

Marge's laugh sounded forced, too quick. "She ran because there was a contract on her and your dear old dad. There's no treasure. It's all family legend. None of it's true." But did a hint of uncertainty lurk beneath the dismissal? "Besides, she wouldn't know, anyway. She was never part of the real family."

His gaze darted from her gun to Townsend's surprised expression. Might his desperate bluff work? "Really? What's the offshore bank account for? The numbers are in the box."

He was flying blind now, making up details and praying they sounded convincing. Sweat beaded on his forehead as he awaited any sign of doubt.

Yes! Uncertainty flickered across her features. The gun wavered in her grip.

"And my grandmother would never let you ruin her efforts," Dylan pressed, standing up straighter despite his terror. Something was shifting inside him, a growing certainty that felt like warmth spreading through his chest. "She spent years trying to make amends. She won't let you destroy everything she built."

"I am a Marino," Marge snarled, but defensiveness now entered her words. "I will take over. She can't do anything to stop me."

The warmth in Dylan's chest grew stronger. Now he understood what his mother wanted. Why she'd given him the key. Why she'd brought him back here, even in death. Not to hide from his heritage, but to claim it.

"I am the rightful heir." A conviction he didn't know he

possessed claimed him. "My mother wanted me to come home. To take my place in this family."

For the first time since this nightmare began, Marge looked shaken. Her gun hand trembled as she stared at him, seeing perhaps not the frightened young man but the legitimate continuation of a bloodline she'd been trying to claim her entire life.

"You think you can just waltz in here and—"

"Down! Now!"

The voice came from behind them, calm in its authority. Dylan glimpsed movement in his peripheral vision; Fr. Phil emerging from the stairwell with the controlled grace of someone trained for combat. His mother's words echoed in Dylan's memory: *Navy SEAL before answering the call to the priesthood.*

Dylan dropped to the concrete floor, his knees hitting hard enough to send pain shooting up his legs. This was all too real. It was childish to believe closing his eyes would make the bullets miss, but he couldn't help squeezing them shut, curling into himself, and waiting for death.

The gunshots came simultaneously, sharp cracks echoing off the basement walls like thunder, one overlapping the other in chaos. Dylan pressed his face against the cold concrete, his whole body shaking as the noise reverberated through his bones.

Then silence.

Terrible, absolute silence that stretched for what felt like hours but couldn't have been more than seconds.

His ears were ringing, and the high-pitched whine made everything else sound muffled and distant. Terrified of what he might see, he opened his eyes and lifted his head.

Blood. Too much blood spread across the concrete in a dark pool that grew larger, spread further even as he watched.

Then he saw Townsend.

The lawyer lay crumpled against the far wall, his expensive suit torn and stained, one hand pressed against his side where crimson seeped between his fingers. His face was gray, his breathing shallow and labored.

Dylan's gaze snapped upward, searching for the source of the chaos. Fr. Phil and Marge were locked in a struggle near the bottom of the stairs. The priest's hands wrapped around her wrist as she fought to bring her gun to bear. Her face twisted, every muscle straining against his grip.

"Stop it! Now!" Dylan scrambled to his feet, his voice cracking.

Something glinted on the concrete near his feet—Townsend's gun, knocked from his grip during the chaos. Dylan lunged for it, his hands shaking as he wrapped his fingers around the grip and pointed it toward the struggling figures.

"You hear that?" Fr. Phil's voice was steady despite the physical struggle, his military training evident in the way he controlled Marge's movements. "Police are on the way. Give it up."

Sirens grew louder. Someone had called for help. Probably someone in the chapel heard the gunshots.

"It's over." Dylan's voice now carried the weight of everything he'd learned about his family, his heritage, and himself.

A profound peace settled over him despite the chaos. The same warmth had filled his chest during his desperate prayer, a certainty that he hadn't been alone in that basement. *Someone* had been guiding his words, giving him strength when he had none left.

Marge's struggle grew weaker. Then she went limp in Fr. Phil's grip. But her eyes, his mother's eyes in a monster's face, remained focused on Dylan with a hatred so pure he stumbled back.

"This isn't over," she whispered the promise that chilled him to the bone. "You have no idea what you've inherited, little nephew. No idea what's coming for you."

Fr. Phil tightened his grip on her wrists. "That's enough."

But was it? Despite the sirens, despite the gun in his hands, despite Fr. Phil's presence, Dylan couldn't shake the feeling....

Marge was right.

This was just the beginning.

CHAPTER 23
FEDERAL RESPONSE, ORLANDO

Ron Peters stared at the same case file he'd been reading for twenty minutes, the words swimming in a blur of bureaucratic sludge and autopsy notes. His third cup of coffee had gone cold hours ago, a bitter film coating the surface like the dread pooling in his gut. Two weeks since the shooting in the chapel basement, and the case was slipping through his fingers like sand.

The fluorescent lights hummed overhead in the covert field office, their harsh white glare making everything look sickly and unreal. Beyond the reinforced windows, the strip mall next door offered a mundane cover for one of the FBI's most classified task forces.

Pizza place, dry cleaner, cell phone repair shop. Nobody walking by would suspect that behind the door marked *Storage Solutions*, some of the nation's most dangerous criminals were being hunted by agents who "didn't" exist.

He rubbed his eyes, feeling the grit of many sleepless nights. The Ghost case had consumed his life for the better part of three years. Now that she'd been captured, he should have been elated. Instead, he was battling complications after complications while the Ghost's lawyers made his life miserable.

His secure phone buzzed with another encrypted message from Quantico. Status update requested on asset placement. Timeline critical. He deleted the message without responding. They'd get their status update when he had something concrete to report, not before.

A sharp knock interrupted his brooding. Nathan Tanner stood in the doorway, his usually crisp appearance showing the strain of two weeks pulling double shifts. The senior agent's tie was loosened, his sleeves rolled up, and his face carried the expression of a man about to deliver news nobody wanted to hear.

"Boss." Tanner's hand grabbed the side of Ron's door.

"Tell me." Ron set down the file, already knowing from his agent's posture that whatever came next wasn't going to improve his day.

"The lawyer died."

The words hit like a physical blow. He had been expecting this call for days, but hearing it still felt like losing a chess piece he couldn't afford to sacrifice. Years of careful relationship building and intelligence gathering, gone in the span of a heartbeat.

He leaned back in his chair, muttering a curse. "I was hoping he'd pull through. When?"

"Four twenty-three this morning. Never regained consciousness." Tanner dropped into the chair across from Ron's desk, exhaustion evident in every movement. "Doc said he would likely have had severe brain injury even if he woke up."

Charles Townsend. The man had been a walking contradiction—criminal and informant, family protector and federal asset. He'd negotiated immunity deals that kept him and his boss, Ralph Marino, out of prison while providing intelligence that dismantled some major criminal operations. Now he was just another casualty in a war most people didn't even know was being fought.

"What's the official cause?" Ron asked, already shifting to damage-control mode.

"Natural causes. Complications from the gunshot wound, brain swelling, cardiac arrest." Tanner consulted his notepad. "No suspicious circumstances. Hospital security footage shows no unauthorized access to his room."

"And unofficially?"

"Unofficially, we lost our primary intelligence source just when we needed him most." Tanner's voice carried the frustration they were all feeling. "Years of inside access, gone. I'd bet the Ghost planned this. You ask me, I think she did it."

Ron stood and walked to the window to face the ordinary. A mother pushing a stroller toward the pizza place, her toddler pointing at something only he could see. An elderly man checking his watch outside the dry cleaner, probably waiting for his wife to finish her shopping. Normal people living normal lives, unaware their safety depended on conversations happening in rooms like this one.

"Walk me through the hospital timeline again." Sometimes, hearing it a second time helped him uncover things he missed.

"Townsend was admitted at 11:47 p.m. the night of the shooting. Emergency surgery lasted four hours. They removed bone fragments and tried to relieve pressure on the brain." Tanner flipped through his notes. "He was stable but unconscious when they moved him to ICU. Round-the-clock monitoring, restricted access, family notification protocols in place."

"Who was listed as next of kin?"

"That's where it gets interesting. Townsend updated his emergency contacts six months ago. Primary contact was listed as Fr. Phil at Holy Angels Chapel."

Ron's eyebrows rose. "The priest? Not family?"

"Apparently, Fr. Phil was the closest thing he had to family.

Sister's been dead for fourteen years, no children, parents long gone."

"He didn't list Marge Beaumont?" Marge, aka the Ghost, was Townsend's niece *on paper*.

"Not according to what I found. Hospital tried to reach him the night of the shooting, but the priest was busy giving statements to local law enforcement."

"So who made the medical decisions?"

"Hospital ethics committee. They had advance directives on file—no extraordinary measures, DNR if brain function was compromised." Tanner's voice carried a note of respect. "Guy was prepared for the worst-case scenario."

Ron turned back to his agent, pieces of a larger puzzle clicking into place. "What's the situation with the prosecutor's office?"

Tanner's expression darkened further. "That's the other complication I mentioned yesterday. Just got off the phone with DA Morrison. He's having serious second thoughts about the murder case."

"We've got two eyewitnesses to a shooting. How is that not enough?" A tight knot twisted in Ron's stomach, the kind that came with too many memos and not enough answers.

"Because neither one actually witnessed the shooting." Tanner opened his notepad to a fresh page. "According to Fr. Phil's statement, he shouted for Dylan to get down, then tackled the Ghost from behind. During the struggle, she managed to get a shot off before he could fully control her weapon. He was focused on her gun hand. He only saw Townsend fall in his peripheral vision."

Ron's jaw tightened. The more he heard about the forensics, the less he liked their chances in court. "And Dylan?"

"Kid dropped to the floor the second he heard Phil's warning. Smart move, saved his life. But he closed his eyes, thinking he'd be shot. He opened his eyes to find Townsend bleeding and a gun on the floor next to him. That's when he picked it up and pointed it at the struggle. So, he can't testify to who fired what or when."

Marge's defense strategy became clear, and Ron didn't like it. Professional criminals didn't survive decades by accident. They survived by being smarter than everyone chasing them.

"Ballistics report?"

"That's where it gets messy." Tanner's voice dropped, taking on the flat, careful tone of someone delivering a diagnosis no one wanted to hear. "The gun Dylan picked up after the shooting? Ballistics confirms it's the one that killed Townsend."

Ron swore under his breath. The coffee turned acidic in his gut; the bitterness climbing higher than his patience.

"And Dylan's prints are the only clear ones on it," Tanner added. "Complete set—both hands. Forensics says he gripped it tight, probably didn't know how to handle a firearm, so he smeared any other trace evidence. No partials, no secondary prints they could lift."

Ron paced back to his desk, gears turning. "She planned this."

"Maybe. But here's the twist," Tanner added. "The Ghost's weapon was found about three feet away. Also fired. That bullet went into the ceiling, trajectory consistent with a wild shot or one made during a struggle."

He narrowed his eyes. "So what's she claiming?"

"She says Townsend pulled a gun on her. They were arguing over the evidence box. Both weapons drawn. She claims Fr. Phil warned Dylan to duck right before things exploded. She fired, missed, bullet went up. She says Townsend fired, and in the chaos, someone shot him. She doesn't say who."

"And no one saw the actual shot?"

"Fr. Phil was trying to stop the fight. He didn't see the critical moment. Just flashes. It happened fast. Two guns drawn. Two rounds fired. Dylan's prints are the only ones intact on the murder weapon. But ballistics can't determine which gun fired first or even whose shot struck Townsend first, assuming both fired."

Ron leaned against his desk, jaw tight. "So she could argue self-defense... or make it look like Dylan panicked and pulled the trigger."

Tanner nodded. "And there's just enough evidence and just enough missing for either story to hold in court."

"And the prosecutor's buying this?"

"DA Morrison's worried about reasonable doubt. Says any halfway decent defense attorney could make Dylan look like the perpetrator instead of the victim." Tanner closed his notepad. "Grieving young man discovers family secrets, family lawyer threatens him with a gun, and chaos ensues. Jury might buy it."

The irony wasn't lost on Ron. Dylan was a victim, of circumstances, of family history, of being in the wrong place at the wrong time with people who'd been playing a deadly game since before he was born. But if the Ghost's version became the official record, Dylan would spend the rest of his life under a cloud of suspicion for a murder he didn't commit.

"We can't let her walk on a murder charge," Ron said, more to himself than to Tanner. "Not when we're this close to understanding her full operation."

"What are you thinking?"

Ron's secure phone buzzed with an incoming priority message from Quantico. The display showed a red flag classification—the kind that usually meant his day was about to get more complicated.

"Federal charges." He pocketed the phone without reading the message. "Terrorism, conspiracy, weapons trafficking, anything we can make stick at the federal level."

"You think Homeland will bite?"

"They will when they understand what we're dealing with." Ron moved toward the door; Tanner on his heels.

"Hernandez, do a deep dive on Dylan and his parents. School records, employment history, financial records, social media presence, the works."

José Hernandez looked up from his computer. "Aren't his folks all..." Seeing Tanner's headshake, Hernandez gave a firm nod. "On it, boss."

Ron glanced back at Tanner. "The Ghost's organization is still monitoring Dylan for a reason. I need to know why before they make their next move."

"You think we missed something?"

"I think a woman who's evaded capture for thirty years doesn't stick around for a family reunion unless she wants something."

"Eh, boss!" Hernandez called. "Assistant Director Lang would like a word. On SCIF."

The secure communication room was a testament to government paranoia and cutting-edge technology. Soundproof walls lined with copper mesh to prevent electronic surveillance, biometric locks that required retinal scans and palm prints, and air gaps that made hacking virtually impossible.

Ron had spent more hours in rooms like this than he cared to count, discussing threats that existed in the shadows between classified briefings and congressional oversight.

The encrypted connection took thirty seconds to establish. When Assistant Director Stan Lang's face appeared on the wall-mounted screen, his expression told Ron everything he needed to know about how the morning would unfold.

"Ron." Conversations happening far above their pay grades weighted Stan's voice. "We need to talk."

"Stan." The two of them had known each other for years.

Neither stood for formality. "I assume this is about our guest in custody?"

"Among other things." Stan consulted something off-screen. "What's your assessment of the local murder case?"

"Shaky. Prosecutor's office is concerned about reasonable doubt. Defense will argue the kid shot Townsend during a family dispute."

"That's what I was afraid of." Stan's face set into grim lines. "New intelligence has come to light. Our friends over at Langley have an operative, Phoenix. Perhaps you've heard of him. He has provided information about the Ghost's... insurance policy."

Ron had indeed. For all any of them knew, Phoenix could be a she, however minuscule the chances were, but he didn't debate that. If Phoenix was talking about insurance policies, the stakes just escalated beyond anything they'd imagined.

"What kind of insurance?"

"The kind that gets the commander in chief's personal attention at six in the morning." Stan leaned closer to the camera. "We can't discuss details over this connection, but I'm authorized to tell you she's acquired something from overseas. Something that could kill thousands if deployed correctly."

"How long do we have?"

"Unknown. Phoenix believes the Ghost will use it as leverage if she thinks she's going down." Stan's voice took on the tone reserved for existential threats. "Psychology profile suggests she'd rather go out in a blaze of glory than spend life in prison."

The familiar responsibility settled on Ron's shoulders like lead armor. Years in law enforcement taught him one hard truth: Worst-case scenarios had a way of becoming reality. A terrorist with access to biological weapons and nothing left to lose was the kind of nightmare that didn't stay on paper.

"What are my orders?"

"Keep her contained. Work every federal angle you can find.

Homeland's already drafting terrorism charges." Stan checked something off camera again. "And, Ron? Phoenix reports the organization is monitoring the Roche kid. This isn't over, not by a long shot."

"Understood." Ron's blood ran cold. "Any word on resources?"

"Whatever you need. NSA's providing signals intelligence, DEA's sharing their international trafficking files, and even Secret Service is contributing protective assets." Stan's expression remained grave. "Everyone understands what's at stake here."

"What about the family? They have a right to know they're still in danger."

"That's being handled through other channels. Your job is to make sure the Ghost never gets the chance to use what she's acquired."

The connection ended, leaving Ron alone with what he'd learned. The Ghost wasn't a mere criminal. She was a terrorist with access to weapons that could devastate entire cities. And somehow, a young man who'd just wanted to learn about his family had stumbled into the middle of it all.

Now, it was up to him to make sure Dylan Roche lived long enough to appreciate his family legacy.

The bullpen was abuzz when Ron returned from the secure communication room. Agents hunched over computers, following digital trails across continents. Phone conversations in multiple languages murmured low as international law enforcement agencies shared intelligence. The organized chaos of a major operation spinning up to full speed.

Tanner appeared at Ron's elbow as they approached the office. "How'd it go with the AD?"

"About as well as expected. The Ghost's got a bioweapon. Engineered pathogen with an antidote she controls. Phoenix confirms the Ghost will use it as leverage if she thinks she's going down."

Tanner went pale. "How many casualties are we talking about?"

"Potentially thousands or millions"—as the latter word stuck in his throat, Ron cleared it to continue—"depending on deployment method and location. Local DA's going to cave on the murder charges. Federal terrorism charges are our only shot at keeping her locked up."

"And if that doesn't work?"

"It'll work." Failure wasn't an option.

"Kyle called. Left a message, 'The chick has hatched.' Said you'd understand."

Ron nodded. "I do." He mentally reviewed all the moving pieces of an operation that would either save innocent lives or get them all killed trying. The Ghost had been playing a long game for decades, but Ron had been preparing for this moment almost as long.

Game on.

CHAPTER 24
THE INTERMEDIARY

The thunder arrived first, a low rumble that seemed to rise from the earth itself before the rain began its assault on St. Agnes's stained glass windows.

Fr. Phil closed the tabernacle and turned around to face the faithful. The weekly Eucharistic Exposition was worth it. More and more people were showing up every week. He went to the sacristy, changed out of his ceremonial garb, and returned to the chapel.

Lightning split the darkness outside, throwing fractured rainbows across the worn wooden pews. The red sanctuary lamp flickered and cast dancing shadows that seemed to breathe with the storm.

The chapel now held maybe half a dozen parishioners, those who stayed after Exposition to continue their prayer. Mrs. Kowalski clutched her rosary in the third pew, her lips moving silently. Mr. Fu sat motionless near the back, staring at the crucifix with the kind of deep contemplation Fr. Phil had come to recognize in veterans who found peace in this sacred space.

When he returned to his office and checked his messages, one with no caller ID requested a confession in an hour. Though confession requests weren't unusual, the artificially distorted voice roused suspicions. This wasn't a plea for absolution. It was something else.

Forty-seven minutes later, he retrieved his purple stole from the sacristy. The silk, cool against his palms, still carried the faint scent of incense from the Benediction. Beyond the sacristy window, the confessional's amber light glowed, occupied.

He slipped into the priest's side of the booth, the cramped space familiar. St. Agnes hadn't gotten around to installing the new reconciliation room yet. People were still using the old confessional booths. The ghosts of countless whispered sins lingered. Fr. Phil pulled the grille open with a soft click.

"Bless me, Father, for I have sinned."

He didn't need the scant silhouette. He recognized Ron's voice. "Ron, I should have known it was you. What's with the cloak-and-dagger?"

"Need to keep up appearances. Nobody suspects anything when I'm here for confession." Ron dropped his voice to a whisper. "These booths aren't exactly soundproof."

"Neither are your Bureau offices, apparently."

"Fair point." A pause. "I've selected Townsend's replacement."

Fr. Phil's stomach dropped. "Already? Ron, the man's barely cold."

"The work doesn't pause for grief. Carol needs someone she can trust, someone to maintain the connection with us."

"You have someone in mind?"

"Agent with the right background. Psychology degree, criminal justice experience. Young enough that Carol won't see her as a threat. New enough to the Bureau that she won't carry baggage from previous operations."

"How new are we talking?"

"Twenty-six. Just finished her probationary period."

"She's around Dylan's age."

"Exactly why it works. Carol just needs someone to serve as a liaison. Check under your seat."

Fr. Phil felt around until his fingers found the manila envelope. Thick. Substantial. Lives reduced to paperwork and photographs.

"What does she know?"

"Everything she needs to. Nothing she doesn't."

"That's not an answer."

A rustle came as Ron shifted. "High enough. She knows about the Ghost situation, the Marino family connections, and the terms of our arrangement with Carol."

"And Dylan?"

"What about him?"

"If he agrees to stay, will you use him?"

"Haven't decided yet. But the kid deserves a normal life. Although I don't know how having the Ghost as his aunt will give him that."

Lightning illuminated the chapel beyond the confessional, followed by thunder that seemed to shake the old building's foundations. Mrs. Kowalski's voice rose in her prayers.

"What about what happened that night? Does she know about the box? And what Dylan found?"

"She'll know what serves the mission. Nothing more."

"Ron—"

"Will you please just review it and let me know?"

"Sure."

The confessional fell silent except for the storm's percussion against the windows. Footsteps left. Then Ron's voice projected clearly across the chapel: "Thank you, Father."

For the benefit of Mrs. Kowalski and Mr. Chen, no doubt.

⁕

Back in the rectory, Fr. Phil poured three fingers of Irish whiskey —a gift from a parishioner who understood that even priests sometimes needed stronger comfort than prayer alone could provide. The amber liquid caught the lamplight as he settled behind his desk, the manila envelope centered like an altar offering.

Rain pelted the rectory windows in sheets, creating rivers that distorted the streetlights beyond. He said a brief prayer for wisdom, then opened the envelope with the precision of a man who'd once defused improvised explosives.

The photograph hit him first. A young woman with intelligent eyes and an expression that managed to be both guarded and open. She looked like she belonged in a college lecture hall, not in the shadow world of federal operations.

Eva Higgins. Age: 26. Born: Grand Rapids, Michigan. Raised: Orlando, Florida. Psychology degree, criminal justice minor. FBI Agent, recently completed probationary period.

Phil scanned the biographical details. Middle child of five. Father worked construction. Mother taught elementary school. Clean service record with the Bureau. Specialized training in behavioral analysis and liaison work. No red flags. No criminal associations. No debts that might compromise her.

The kind of agent who'd earned her position through merit, not connections.

He found the flash drive tucked into the envelope's corner, a device no larger than his thumb that probably contained enough classified information to end several careers. Phil plugged it into his laptop and waited as encrypted files populated the screen.

The first video file opened with Ron's voice: "This is Special Agent Peters conducting a performance review interview with Agent Eva Higgins regarding specialized assignment candidacy."

Higgins sat in a standard federal conference room—beige walls, fluorescent lighting, institutional furniture that had seen better decades. Her posture was professional but relaxed, hands folded on the table, and her navy blazer spoke of Bureau dress codes rather than department store sales.

"What draws you to this particular assignment?" Ron asked from off camera.

"The complexity. Working with someone like Carol requires understanding trauma responses, building trust with someone who has every reason to be suspicious of federal agents." Higgins's voice carried quiet confidence. "My background in behavioral analysis and recent training have prepared me for this kind of sensitive liaison role."

Fr. Phil nodded. Professional. Not seasoned yet, but her response showed good instincts.

"How do you assess this assignment's risks?"

"Carol's going to be naturally suspicious of anyone new in her circle. She's protective of her family, especially after everything that's happened. The key is being genuine about my role as liaison. I'm there to facilitate communication between her and the task force, not to spy or manipulate."

"That's the approach we need, although some duties may come later." A beat. "You know who Dylan is?"

"Yes, he's Carol's newfound grandson."

He watched several more clips. Her responses remained consistent—thoughtful, grounded, with an idealism that hadn't yet been ground down by bureaucracy. When Ron asked about undercover work, she didn't flinch.

"If it protects innocent people, yes. But I'd want clear parameters. I wouldn't want to make things worse for the people I'm trying to help."

An impressive answer. Too many agents thought like operators instead of protectors.

The final video offered grainy footage from a coffee shop surveillance camera. Higgins sat across from a young man—Kyle Peters, Ron's son.

"So your dad's really FBI?" Higgins stirred sugar into her coffee.

Kyle laughed, his chest swelling even as he ducked his head and rubbed the back of his neck. "Yeah, but it's not as exciting as you'd think. He doesn't bring home classified briefings or anything. Mostly, it's paperwork and surveillance. Not exactly *Mission: Impossible.*"

"But still." Higgins's eyes lit up. "He's like a real agent, right? I mean, he can't tell you everything, but some of the places he's traveled…"

Kyle glanced around the coffee shop, then leaned closer. "He can't talk about most of it. But he's worked with some serious people. Organized crime, international stuff. The cases that make the news years later when they can release the details."

"That must be incredible." She nudged aside her cup, arms folded against the tabletop. "Knowing you're making a real difference. Standing between dangerous people and innocent victims."

"You thinking about applying?" Kyle grinned. "Dad's always looking for good people."

Higgins laughed but tipped her head in genuine consideration. "I don't know if I'm cut out for that kind of life. But, yeah, sometimes I think about it."

She was quiet, watching steam rise from her cup. "My freshman year, there was this girl in my dorm. Sarah Martinez. Sweet kid, studying to be a teacher. She had this boyfriend who seemed great at first—flowers, romantic dinners, the whole shebang."

Kyle's coffee mug stilled halfway between the table and his mouth.

"Then he started isolating her. Made her drop her sorority, quit her part-time job. Said she didn't need friends because she had him. By spring semester, she was covered in bruises she tried to hide with makeup." Higgins's shoulders drooped. "I reported it to campus security, the local police, even tried to get her family involved. Everyone said they couldn't do anything without her cooperation. The system failed her because it was designed to react, not prevent."

"What happened to her?"

"She transferred schools. Never heard from her again." Higgins raised her chin. "But that's when I knew I wanted to be part of something that could help people *before* it was too late."

When the video ended, Fr. Phil sat in the quiet, whiskey untouched. Rain continued its assault on the study windows, and somewhere in the distance, a siren wailed through the night.

His secure phone chimed.

"Phil here."

"Knew you'd dive right in." Ron's voice carried the satisfaction of a man whose plans were proceeding on schedule. "Thoughts?"

"She's impressive. Smart, principled, grounded. But nothing in here says she's ready."

"She doesn't need to be ready. She needs to be believable."

"Ron—"

"Carol's being told she's getting a new administrative assistant. Recent graduate, eager to learn. The kind of earnest young woman who wouldn't know tradecraft if it bit her."

"Okay, what about Dylan?"

"He doesn't need to know anything beyond what he already knows."

Phil exhaled. "All right. I'll talk to Carol tomorrow."

"Good. One more thing. I need you to confirm what you saw that night."

The question Fr. Phil had been dreading. He closed his eyes, letting the memory play out again. The chapel cellar. The Ghost's finger on the trigger. His own desperate lunge to disarm her.

"I told you before. I tried to stop her. She got one shot off. Went into the ceiling, I think. I was focused on her gun hand."

"What do you think happened? Who shot whom?"

He visualized that scene. "I tackled her after she fired, I believe. She dropped the gun but picked it up again. Now, there's a chance she picked up a different gun. If Townsend was shot first, he fell and dropped his gun. So, it's plausible she picked up that gun. But I can't say for sure."

"You don't think Townsend did it?"

"He changed, Ron. He wouldn't shoot his niece. And he wouldn't let anything happen to Dylan."

"You're certain Dylan didn't fire?"

"Positive. The kid dropped flat when I yelled the warning. He was in shock. When he picked up the weapon afterward, he held it like it might explode. Kid's never fired a gun in his life."

"That matches the forensics. Talk soon."

The line went dead.

Outside, St. Agnes's bell tower chimed midnight. Somewhere in the distance, a car door slammed, and footsteps echoed on wet pavement.

The sanctuary lamp flickered in the chapel beyond, casting dancing shadows that seemed to nod in agreement. Outside, the storm moved on, leaving the eerie calm that always preceded the real chaos.

And in the silence, Fr. Phil, former Navy SEAL, current priest, and reluctant keeper of too many dangerous secrets, prayed for guidance to do the right thing.

CHAPTER 25

INHERITANCE

Dylan straightened his new tie—still cheaper than what most executives probably wore, but at least it wasn't from a thrift store. The Orlando skyline stretched beyond the floor-to-ceiling window, afternoon sunlight warming the executive office that still felt surreal. He shifted in the leather chair, the mahogany desk gleaming under the overhead lights.

"I bet you never thought you'd be sitting at *that* desk." From the plush couch, Tommy propped his sneakers on the coffee table. "I mean, look at you—an actual dress shirt that fits, pants without holes. You even combed your hair."

Dylan ran a hand through his hair, messing it up again. Three weeks ago, he'd been dodging calls from debt collectors and eating ramen for dinner. Now, his debts were gone, wiped clean with a single wire transfer from Carol.

"The suit's from a department store." He shrugged. "Carol offered to take me shopping somewhere fancy, but... you know, that's not me."

The air-conditioning hummed, mixing with the distant sounds of traffic below. Tommy stretched his arms behind his head, grinning like he'd won the lottery. "You know what your job is yet?"

"Management's being vague. Something about 'learning the business from the ground up'." Dylan opened his desk drawer, still surprised to find actual office supplies instead of the broken staplers and dried-out pens from his old job. "They're supposed to call Ken, get a reference. What about you? Is it official?"

Tommy's grin widened. He pulled out his phone, waggling it. "Got the email two days ago. Staff accountant, M&M Enterprises. How's she handling everything? Your grandmother? About the Ghost?"

Dylan's jaw tightened. The smell of fresh coffee from the break room down the hall drifted in, but it couldn't mask the bitter taste that came with thoughts of his mother's twin. "She's devastated. Finding out her daughter, the one she thought was dead, was alive and running a criminal empire..." He rubbed his temples. "The Ghost won't see her. Won't see anyone."

"Probably for the best."

Outside, a siren wailed, then faded. Dylan stood and walked to the window, his reflection ghostlike against the glass.

"I guess your hope to find your roots came true," Tommy said.

Dylan pressed his palm against the cool window. "Yeah. Just not how I expected." He traced his face's reflection. "Mom left me more than just her eyes and her stubborn streak. She left me a responsibility." He straightened his shoulders, the weight of his new role settling like the new suit. "To carry on the legacy."

A MONTH LATER

The morning dew clung to Dylan's dress shoes as he stepped between the headstones. Birds chirped in the oak trees overhead, their songs breaking the cemetery's stillness. He stopped before two graves, one weathered and moss-stained, the other bearing fresh-carved letters that caught the early sunlight.

He knelt and placed the white lilies at the base of the newer stone. "Well, you're finally together again."

The scent of damp earth and grass filled his nostrils as he stood, brushing dirt from his slacks. With Carol's blessing and financial help, he had his mother's remains moved here. They barely had five years together in life, but now they'd rest side by side forever.

Fr. Phil's words echoed in his mind: *"Last I heard, he had a good job in Atlanta."* The priest had blinked when Dylan pressed him about revealing he'd kept in touch. *"Well, let's just say your father let me know his forwarding address."*

So the priest had been in contact with his parents, at least initially. Maybe he'd helped them more than Dylan would ever know.

"Mom, Dad, I nearly got myself killed." His voice carried

across the empty cemetery. "The Ghost—you know, your evil twin—had this twisted plan. I know now why you both ran." A breeze rustled the oak leaves above. "I'm living at the Mirror Estate. Can you believe that? Though I got an apartment in the city too, closer to work."

A squirrel darted between headstones.

"They gave me some fancy title at the hotel, but I'm learning the ropes. Management trainee with delusions of grandeur." The joke fell flat in the morning air. "Agent Peters wants my help tracking down the last of the criminal network's people. I said yes."

He crouched again, running his fingers along his mother's smooth granite headstone.

"First stop's Hong Kong. Tommy's coming with me." He stood and straightened his tie. "We're going to clean this mess up. All of it."

The sun climbed higher and warmed his back through his shirt. Somewhere, a lawn mower started up, distant and rhythmic.

"I'm gonna make you proud."

He stepped back from the graves, his shadow falling across both stones. The weight that had pressed on his chest for weeks now lifted with each breath. He strode toward the cemetery gates, his footsteps steady on the gravel path, leaving his parents to their eternal rest.

Living Secrets, the next gripping installment in the Mirror Estate series, is available on Amazon and Kindle Unlimited. Grab it now!

THANK YOU!

Thank you for diving into *Buried Secrets*! Writing this story has been such a wild ride and knowing that you've spent time with the cast means the world to me.

I hope you loved reading it as much as I loved writing it. If you'd be so kind as to leave a review on Amazon and/or Goodreads to share your impressions with others, I would greatly appreciate it. Your insights will help other readers find the book.

BONUS EXTENDED EPILOGUE

KYLE

Kyle Peters shifted in his seat. Just what had he done to land on a US senator's radar? Let alone *this* senator?

Simon Roth wasn't just another polished politician. He sat on the Intelligence Committee. Rumor had it he was the front-runner for his party's presidential nomination.

This was Kyle's second week of his first assignment as a full-fledged FBI Special Agent.

Had he already blown it?

What would he tell Dad if he got fired just after his probationary period?

"The senator is ready for you now."

A voice snapped him out of his spiral. Kyle's pulse kicked up. He stood too fast, nearly knocking his chair over. "Thanks."

The local office wasn't big, although he imagined the senator's office in DC would be more impressive. He strode past two offices and a conference room, with a long table where a few people were milling around, and headed to the senator's corner office.

Senator Roth surprised him by standing at the door, his hand out and his smile polished. "Come on in, Kyle."

"Senator." They shook hands.

Senator Roth went behind his desk and sat down. "Have a seat, please."

Kyle sat. "You wanted to see me, sir?"

"Yes, I didn't mean for him to scare you. Nothing to worry about. I need a favor. A trusted friend pointed me to you."

At that unexpected revelation, he didn't know what to say.

The senator continued. "I understand you have been to Hong Kong?"

"Yes, I stayed there for about two months, or rather six weeks, with my dad once when he had an assignment at the consulate. And I visited there again with a friend and her family."

"And the friend would be Eva Higgins?"

Whoa, they do know everything! "Yes."

The senator nodded. "How would you like to visit the city again?"

EVA

Contrary to what Eva Higgins expected, the walking path connecting the hotels to Universal Studios was nearly empty. Just the occasional jogger and a family dragging souvenir bags. Maybe most tourists preferred the water taxis. Or the shuttle buses. Or maybe they didn't feel like walking alone in the humid Orlando air.

A lone figure sat on a shaded bench ahead, checking his phone.

"Training go well?" The man she knew only as "Uncle Bill" spoke without looking up.

"Tough." She stopped in front of him. "But I survived." The training ended long ago. Last week, she finished her time as a probationary agent in Atlanta. Her next posting was back home in Orlando.

"You should sit."

She sat and waited. In all the times they met, Uncle Bill always took the initiative to talk.

"This is your last chance to back out."

She had thought long and hard about her situation. "I'm doing it."

A flicker of a smile touched his face. He dropped a flash drive into her purse. "Everything we have on the Marino family. Study it. The grandson has a sidekick, someone also around your age. You'll blend in, earn their trust, keep me updated."

Eva hesitated. "Still no word from Mr. Peters."

"You'll hear from him."

He stood, wiping the sweat off his forehead.

"Be careful." He walked off without looking back.

KYLE

"You want me to fly to Hong Kong and escort a girl, Lily Tso, back here?" Kyle frowned at the photo the senator showed him, a girl in her late teens. This didn't sound like something the FBI trained him for.

Senator Roth nodded, eyes locked on a distant point on the wall. For a second, he didn't even seem to be in the room.

"Sir?"

The senator blinked, then refocused. "Right. Yes. That's part of the mission. The rest is in the folder." He gestured to the manila file on the desk. "Report to the consulate. An attaché will brief you once you arrive."

Kyle reached for the folder, but hesitated. Was that his cue to leave?

He rose to his feet.

"Kyle, as of this moment, you're on loan to me as an intelligence officer. I've already cleared it with your director. Everything in that folder and everything the attaché tells you is strictly need-to-know."

Kyle's heart thumped. Intelligence officer? On loan to a senator?

"Yes, sir."

"Keep her safe." Roth paused, probably noticing Kyle's confused look. "Stay current. There's unrest in Hong Kong. Most of the demonstrators are teens and young adults."

That gave Kyle pause. Lily Tso wasn't just a random young woman. He could feel it.

"Yes, sir." He turned to go.

"One more thing."

He stopped midstep.

Roth held out a slip of paper. "This number's not in the folder. Memorize it. It's your contact when you return or if everything goes sideways."

Kyle slipped it into his jacket. "Understood."

EVA

Half an hour later, Eva was back in the motel, staring at the laptop screen. She had plugged the drive in and was working through the decryption.

For Your Eyes Only.

That was the first thing she saw when the file opened. *Cute, very James Bond.*

Uncle Bill had been right. Agent Peters, *Mr.* Peters to her no more, had contacted her fifteen minutes ago. Their meeting was set for tomorrow morning.

After the call, she'd paced her motel room for a solid five minutes, muttering, "You can do this," like a mantra. Only when the adrenaline wore off did she plug in the flash drive.

The long but compelling document opened with the Marino

family's history, legitimate roots, surprisingly. Then something shifted between the wars. They'd gone dark: gambling, racketeering, prostitution. But none of it violent, at least not at first.

When did they make the leap to human trafficking? She scrolled past pages of coded operations and blurred photos.

A knock startled her.

She slammed the laptop shut, heart thudding.

Then came the voice. "You gonna open the door? Or should I just leave your food on the floor?"

She exhaled. Kyle.

She swung the door wide open so he could walk through with a carryout bag. "How did your meeting go?"

He put the bag on the desk. "He didn't fire me. I've been temporarily reassigned. And I'll be out of reach for a bit."

"Out of reach?" She closed the door, then helped him set the food out.

"Going overseas."

"Oh, for how long?" She took a burrito bowl and sat on the bed facing the desk.

"No idea. A few days, maybe." He grabbed a large burrito and settled in the chair. "That's why I came to say hi before you start your assignment."

"You know something I don't?"

"Of course not! I just figured they sent you here for a reason.... Hmm, this is good. Anyway, they didn't send you here to go to Universal Studios. I don't know the details of Dad's work, but I know his office is here."

"We're meeting tomorrow. Let's hope he's not making me do intern work."

"I wouldn't know, although I doubt it. Probably some mundane assignment."

More like, definitely not. But she kept her mouth shut.

Kyle was her best friend. They'd known each other since their teens. He'd crushed on her back then, hard. That phase didn't last. Once he realized she saw him as a brother, not a boyfriend, he'd pivoted. Declared her his surrogate sister.

"What's up?" He eyed her. "You're not yourself."

"Am I doing the right thing?"

"About?"

"Well, you know, trying to impress your dad so he'd pull strings to get me into the agency. All that."

"Hey, Dad wouldn't do that if he didn't think you were capable. Don't sell yourself short."

"You're right."

They ate in silence.

"Be patient. You'll get justice for your aunt." Kyle tossed the wrapper into the wastebasket.

That came out of nowhere. "What are you talking about?"

He looked right at her. "I know you. Your aunt's disappearance impacted you. And you want justice. That's why you grabbed the chance to join the Bureau."

"You really know me."

"Of course." He got up and opened his arms to hug her. "I leave later this evening. I'll see you."

LIVING SECRETS

A Thriller

BOOK 2
SNEAK PEEK

CHAPTER 1

USA/CHINA

"Status?" the Ghost demanded.

"He needs more convincing."

"Use leverage. Anything. Make him cooperate. We've got friends in that part of China. The triads owe us. Call them in if you have to."

Silence for a beat.

"You're not really planning to use his notes, are you? We don't have the resources to build something like that. And the Chinese won't appreciate you hijacking their research "

"That's not your concern. Get it done." She ended the call.

Marge Beaumont, the Ghost, leaned back in her chair. She'd watched the video in secret, footage smuggled out of a hidden Chinese lab.

A grotesque display—test subjects convulsing, bleeding, dying.

The scientist behind the camera had promised a perfect storm—smallpox, cholera, Ebola rolled into one.

Without the antidote, death was inevitable. The timer ran forty-eight to ninety-six hours.

One hundred percent fatal.

She'd shuddered when she watched it. Now, the memory hardened her resolve. She needed that bargaining chip.

CHAPTER 2

MIRROR ESTATE

Dylan Roche sat at his cluttered desk, thumbing through a set of handwritten notes. Even in these photocopies, the faded ink hinted at secrets and mysteries buried deep within his family history. The past couple of months had shaken him to the core. Now, he sought answers, resolution, and perhaps even closure.

His fingertips traced the notes' outlines. These had once belonged to his grandfather, a decorated police officer in the organized crime unit. The FBI now held the originals as evidence, but he'd made copies before handing those over to FBI Special Agent Ron Peters. Dylan had to protect himself, to have something tangible to hold onto as he ventured down this treacherous path.

But now, at this crossroad of his investigation, he needed more help, a connection to his roots, to the fragments of his shattered family.

"Fr. Phil," Dylan muttered. The priest knew more than he revealed. After all, Dylan's mother had entrusted the priest to deliver her email to him after her death.

He put the papers away and pushed to his feet to head to the chapel, a short walk from the estate.

His phone rang. Agent Peters's contact flashed onto the screen.

Dylan answered. It was a short conversation. Fr. Phil would have to wait.

ABOUT THE AUTHOR

S.F. Baumgartner writes fast-paced Christian suspense thrillers. Book 1 of her Mirror Estate series, Living Secrets, was selected as one of the Top Picks in the thriller category at Killer Nashville, 2024. Her love for writing comes second only to her love of reading.

When she's not busy writing about complex characters, secretive operatives, and relentless agents, she spends her time binge-watching crime TV shows, such as NCIS, or playing with her cats. If you enjoy James Patterson's style—specifically short chapters—you'll love her Mirror Estate series.

To be the first to know about any sales, promotions, and new releases, sign up for our monthly newsletter. By subscribing, you'll stay informed about all the latest happenings and never miss an opportunity to explore this captivating world.

ALSO BY
S.F. BAUMGARTNER

Mirror Estates series

Buried Secrets, book 1

Living Secrets, book 2

Forgotten Secret, book 3

Tangled Secrets, book 4

Hidden Secrets, book 5

Shadowed Secret, book 6

Stolen Secret, book 7

Box Set (Books 1-4)

KC & Orlando Prime series

Christmas Murders, a prequel

Fatal Invitation, book 1

ACKNOWLEDGMENTS

Publishing a novel is not a solo endeavor, and I'm deeply grateful to those who made this book possible.

A heartfelt thanks to Deirdre Lockhart at Brilliant Cut Editing and Chelsea Lauren from Represent Publishing for their invaluable guidance and support.

A special thanks must also be extended to Brittany Evans, the talented graphic designer, who transformed my vision into the stunning cover that graces this edition. Her creativity and skill have truly brought the book to life, and I am in awe of her work.

I also want to thank the amazing beta and ARC readers—your feedback and enthusiasm were crucial in refining this novel.

To my family, your unwavering support has been my greatest strength. And finally, to you, dear readers—this book is for you. Enjoy the journey!